Nonsense

The Senseless Series, Volume 3

W.J. May

Published by Dark Shadow Publishing, 2015.

Nonsense
(Senseless Series Book III)
By W.J. May
Copyright 2015 W.J. May

Also by W.J. May

Blood Red Series
Courage Runs Red
The Night Watch

Daughter of Darknes: Victoria's Journey
Huntress

Daughters of Darkness: Victoria's Journey
Victoria

Hidden Secrets Saga
Seventh Mark - Part 1
Seventh Mark - Part 2
Marked By Destiny
Compelled

The Chronicles of Kerrigan
Rae of Hope
Dark Nebula
House of Cards
Royal Tea
Under Fire

The Hidden Secrets Saga
Seventh Mark (part 1 & 2)

The Senseless Series
Radium Halos
Radium Halos - Part 2
Nonsense

Standalone
Shadow of Doubt (Part 1 & 2)
Five Shades of Fantasy
Glow - A Young Adult Fantasy Sampler
Shadow of Doubt - Part 1
Shadow of Doubt - Part 2
Four and a Half Shades of Fantasy
Full Moon
Dream Fighter
What Creeps in the Night
Forest of the Forbidden
HuNted
Arcane Forest: A Fantasy Anthology
Ancient Blood of the Vampire and Werewolf

The Senseless Series:

FIND W.J. May

Website: http://www.wanitamay.yolasite.com
Facebook: https://www.facebook.com/pages/Author-WJ-May-FAN-PAGE
Newsletter:
SIGN UP FOR W.J. May's Newsletter to find out about new releases, updates, cover reveals and even freebies!
http://eepurl.com/97aYf

Cover design by: Book Cover by Design
Book II

Description:

Everyone needs to be a hero at one point in their life.

The small town of Elliot Lake will never be the same again. Six friends have become five and one is to blame, leaving the four remaining to pick up the pieces of their lives and try to carry one.

While mourning the death of their friend, Rylee, and dealing with Kieran's betrayal, Zoe, Heidi, Brent, and Seth all go to Mexico with Zoe's father for their winter break. While there, they discover Zoe's father has kept a few secrets of his own, and after Kieran secretly visits, Zoe begins to suspect that there's more to the story of Rylee's death than there seems.

Despite having a good time in Mexico, the past events come back to haunt them when they return to Elliot Lake. With tempers flaring and the sting from Kieran's betrayal still fresh in their minds, the friends begin to doubt if they can even trust each other. As the group begins to fall apart, something dark and sinister makes itself known in Elliot Lake.

Zoe knows she's being followed, but by whom, she's not sure. Kieran tries to solve Rylee's murder to protect his friends, but can only go so far before risking being caught by the police. However, after Heidi is trapped in a robbery, it becomes apparent that they need to stick together and work as a team once again if they ever want to survive.

An incredulous group of heroes. A traitor in the midst. Some dreams are written in blood.

This is book 3 of the Senseless Series. Join Zoe, Brent, Kieran on an epic adventure of supernatural, love, loss and thrilling mystery.

W.J. May

Table of Contents

Chapter 1

Zoe

"You four need a quiet winter break," Dad said, his eyes lingering on me but passing over the four of us. Seth, Heidi, Brent and I sat squeezed into the living room couch at Brent's house. All of our parents stood in the room, silently nodding their heads. "Somewhere warm, away from Elliot Lake."

"I don't really feel like going anywhere." Heidi played with the Kleenex in her hand. "Rylee's dead."

"And Kieran's run off." Brent glanced at me before crushing his fingers into fists.

"I say we hunt him down ourselves," Seth grumbled. His eyes grew wide when he realized he'd said the words aloud.

Brent shot him a warning glare.

"Sweetie." His mother came to the side of the couch and rubbed his shoulder. "There is nothing you kids can do. Let the police do their jobs. They know what they're doing."

My heart filled with adrenalin at Seth's words, ready to race away and hide. No one, except maybe Brent, knew the entire truth of the story. Right now, I had no intention of ever trying to find Kieran.

Dad cleared his throat. "I know a fellow doctor-friend who owns a holiday house in Mexico. It's in a small city, away from the big tourist places, but near some great Aztec ruins. It's safe, like a fortress. It'll make for a quiet week, with some healthy sunshine. I've already booked the time off work and can take you guys down there." He glanced at the other parents who nodded. "All your folks agreed. There's one catch..."

No parents? Well, except for Dad. Maybe it was time we let him in on our little secret.

All four of us must have had the same thought run through our heads. "Let's go," we all said at the same time.

Dad laughed. "That was easy. Aren't any of you concerned about the 'catch'?" He stood and clapped his hands. "We leave tomorrow morning at four thirty. Flight takes off at seven."

Seth groaned.

So did I, apparently none of us had been sleeping much the past week and a half. *Had it really been a week since Rylee died? Since Kieran left?* Part of me was relieved but the other half, the broken one, missed him. I was torn at what to think or do. I had no one to talk to about it either. The others were so angry at him and then ticked at me when I just stayed silent in our conversations. I didn't know if I should tell them about Kieran's past or concentrate on the fact that he'd killed Rylee. None of us knew what exactly happened that night – except she had died and he'd run away. *Maybe in Mexico we'll be able to talk and start finding some answers.*

"Zoe-zey?" Dad tapped my knee lightly.

"Yeah?" I blinked, focussing on him.

"How about you sleep at your mom's tonight? I'll pick you up in the morning."

"Sure." I didn't mind. Mom had been awesome the past week. She didn't ask questions or pry, she'd just hand me the box of Kleenexes when my eyes couldn't hold back the dams of flooding tears. It was a nice change of pace from Dad always asking if I was okay, and Brent telling me that he was there whenever I needed him. I knew both of them meant well, but there was nothing I could tell them without causing trouble. Of course, I wasn't okay. One of my best friends had just died, possibly murdered in cold blood by my ex-boyfriend. *Kind of ex-boyfriend.* We never did have an official breakup, and even though I thought it was clear to both of us that it was over, I wasn't sure if Kieran considered us broken up. He had given me the crystal Scottish thistle for safe-keeping, saying he wanted the two things most precious to him to be together. It was in my room right now, still shut in its box, burning a hole through my closet floor, wanting to be taken out and displayed. I wasn't about to set it on my nightstand. The last thing I needed was another reminder of Kieran for me to see any time I looked the wrong way. It would just bring me back to that terrible, terrible night.

The parents started to depart, leaving us to our own devices. I could hear some of them talking outside about us. Seth's dad was telling Heidi's mom that Seth had two therapy appointments this week but had skipped out on both of them. He was worried Seth was going through more than normal grieving over a friend.

What's normal grieving over a friend? It's only been a week since she died. But he was right. There was more going on with Seth. There was more going on with all of us. And if any of us told anybody, even a therapist, about what was going on, then they would have us committed.

"You all right?" Brent mumbled under his breath. No one else in the room could hear him, but the question was directed at me. I tuned out Seth's and Heidi's parents and focused on the steady heart rate of Brent, realizing it was much slower than my own. My shaking hands had tipped him off that everything wasn't all right, and I was about to have my third breakdown this week, just because I thought of Kieran and his stupid Scottish thistle.

"Yeah," I said, leaning against his shoulder. "Just tired." That wasn't a lie. I had barely slept at all since Rylee's death. I just kept dreaming about her mangled lifeless body on the side of the road before seeing Kieran's face at the moment I realized he was a murderer.

Brent put his arm around me and pulled me closer to him. I wrapped my arms around his waist, glad for the quiet comfort.

His face was turned away at an awkward angle and I knew that with his hand on my shoulder, my sweater was now completely see-through to him. I flushed. "It's okay," I said. "I'm wearing a t-shirt under the sweater."

"Thanks," he muttered, turning back to a more natural position. I saw his cheeks rise in color and almost giggled. It was sweet of him to turn away when he was in danger of accidentally seeing something he shouldn't. He couldn't help but gain the ability to see through anything he touched with his hands or feet, but he never tried to abuse that power by attempting to get a peep show.

"I still say we try to hunt down Kieran ourselves," Seth muttered. "That bastard needs to pay!"

"We can't just go out looking for him," Heidi argued. "He knows everything about us, now. We don't even really know his power." She looked at me with accusing eyes but didn't say anything.

None of us even knew he had a power until the day Rylee died. It didn't follow one of the five human senses like ours did. We'd assumed the five of us had gotten heightened senses, and since he hadn't grown up here, it hadn't happened to him. Except he had received an ability. Whether he hid it from the get go or didn't realize he had it, he had one. He had a strange sixth sense. What exactly it was, not even I knew, but I knew that a lot of the time, he could read my mind, and it seemed like he could also see into the future. "Let's just let the police do their work." I sighed. "It's not worth the trouble we'd be in if we conducted our own search. What good will it do anyway? Rylee's not coming back."

"You just want your boyfriend to get away with it." Seth glared at me.

Brent jumped up and faced Seth before I could do anything. "You take that back," he warned. "You don't think Kieran has hurt her, too? She was betrayed just as much as the rest of us. And he was never her boyfriend."

Seth looked ready to say something to Brent and then shook his head. He had the decency to give him a sheepish shrug. He held his hands up in surrender. "Sorry, Zoe. Guess I was a little out of line."

"I'll say." I glowered at him. "Just because I don't want to waste time trying to track a ghost doesn't mean I don't want justice!" I blinked back tears, hating the way my voice cracked. I wondered if it was noticeable to everyone or just me.

"Look, I apologized. What else do you want?" He scowled at me, not looking at all sorry anymore.

"Just leave, Seth," I said. "Get the hell out of my damn house."

He got up instantly, the creak of his chair piercing my ears. "I can smell your guilt a mile away." He stomped out of the house, each footfall sounding like a loud thunderclap.

Silence from Brent and Heidi followed after the door slammed.

"What is happening to us?" Heidi whispered to Brent and I. "We're just falling apart." A tear slid down her cheek.

I sat down, my heart rate slowly returning to normal as my temper cooled. "I'm sorry, guys." I was on the verge of tears myself. "I don't know what came over me."

"I think your dad is right, Zoe," Brent spoke quietly. "We do need to get away from here. The sooner, the better."

Chapter Two

When we flew, no amount of car plugs or swallowing could stop the headache threatening to crack my skull in half. The roar of the engines, the gross sounds of people chewing and drinking, the constant scratch of the pen against a journal's pages from the girl right in front of me, and the typing on a tablet from a middle-aged man two seats up was deafening to me and I stayed awake throughout the whole flight despite the sleeping pill I took before liftoff.

Seth's face remained in a constant grimace from the smells on the plane. The poor guy had to use two of the paper bags stored in the seats in front of us. At least it got Heidi and Brent laughing, even though Heidi had to put her hand over her mouth when the airplane food was served out. I had read somewhere that airplane food was really as good as most other food and it was just the altitude or something messing with our taste buds that made it taste gross, but Heidi's superhuman taste buds were apparently just as affected by the altitude as everyone else's. It was without a doubt one of the worst flights any of us had ever been on, and we were all relieved when we finally landed in Mexico.

As soon as we got to the house I went straight to my room, changed into jogging pants and crawled into bed. My head hurt, I missed Rylee, and worst of all, I longed for Kieran. As much as I tried to fight it, I still missed the comfort of his presence and his musical Scottish accent. But of course, I couldn't tell anyone that so I buried deeper under the covers, wishing I could disappear.

Strange sounds finally woke me. I had no idea how long I'd slept, but the headache had left, only leaving the emptiness in my chest. Kicking away the covers, I took a moment to listen to the noises around me and glance around the room I'd paid little attention to before.

Eccentric sounding birds sang outside which let me know it was probably early morning as the rest of the house was relatively quiet. My dad's soft snoring let me know he was sleeping just down the hall. The ceiling to floor windows gave view to beautiful greenery and a pool. The bright room had the large bed, a dresser and a desk on the far side. The artwork seemed hand painted with bright coral red and turquoise colors. It was all gorgeous. It felt like paradise compared to my room back home. It was almost as if I was in some sort of fantasy, and the real world was a long way away. *Rylee would have loved this place.* I smiled, imagining her lounging around in a bikini on the beach, trying to seduce her next conquest and doing so with plenty of ease. I blinked back tears. *You're on a vacation, Zoe. You're supposed to be having fun, not mourning. You think Rylee wants you moping in your room when you're in Mexico?* I smiled. She definitely would not.

I unpacked my suitcase and changed into a bathing suit. I'd slept for over fifteen hours according to my watch. *No way am I going back to bed.* I slipped on a long white t-shirt and listened to my bare feet as they padded across the hardwood floor to the sliding door that led outside.

The heat hit me like a wave. Unlike the humid summers we had back home, this warmth was dry but already hot for six in the morning. The air conditioning inside had hidden the heat perfectly. By the time I'd reached the pool, I'd already stripped off my shirt and tossed it on one of the chaise lounge chairs, ready to dive in.

The water caressed my skin and the quiet under the surface had my ears and head begging to stay down longer. However, my lungs requiring air won over the quietness. I swam lengths of the pool under the water, only coming up for air before quickly dropping back down again. Twenty minutes later, I paused to hang on the concrete wall of the pool.

Brent sat on the chair beside my discarded shirt. He leaned forward, his elbows on his knees and his fingers tapping some new rhythm against the pad of his thumb.

"Head feeling better?"

"Yeah, thanks." I glanced behind him. "Everyone else still sleeping?"

He nodded. "I figured you'd be out here. He stared at me a long time before finally taking a deep breath. "We need to talk."

"What's up?" Using my arms, I lifted myself out of the pool and grabbed a towel. I sat down beside him. "Is it about Kieran?"

"No. Yes." He ran a hand through his hair, quick and rough. "I don't know."

I'd never seen him flustered before. My hand automatically went to his knee and I squeezed it. "Brent, it's me. Just tell me what's going on. Is it something bad?" A weird thought ran through my head. "Did Kieran try to contact you?"

"No!" His cheeks puffed as he blew out a quick breath. His voice softened. "It's not bad. At least, I don't think so. And Kieran's not going to try to contact me. He's dead if he does."

Brent didn't know the whole story. He didn't know what Kieran's dad had done to him. It impacted his entire life and even though he'd killed Rylee, I was beginning to wonder if it had been an accident. The weather had been bad that night. Could he have hit her with his bike by mistake?

"Zoe? Are you listening?" One side of Brent's mouth lifted. "Never thought I'd be saying that to you again after the night in the mine."

I smiled. "Sorry. Guess I kinda got lost in my thoughts for a moment. You said Kieran's never going to come back."

"Sorta. I went by his place before we left. It's all locked up, but I looked inside." He raised his hands and wiggled his fingers. "The place was military clean but a mess in a weird way. Like he left in a hurry. He's running and you only run when you're guilty."

I shivered despite the warm air. "I guess you're right."

Brent's brows knotted together. "You guess? You think he didn't do it? We all know he's guilty. Zoe, you aren't still in love with him are you?" He straightened, the shock on his face impossible to miss. "He's a monster. I mean, I know what you said to Seth, but I know you, Zoe. You're still in love with him."

He didn't know and the others wouldn't understand. The hurt and disappointment in Brent's expression ticked me off. "I know what he did. And I don't need you to judge me." I stood, no longer interested in talking. "I'm going inside to change." I grabbed my shirt and stomped back toward the house.

Pounding barefoot on the interlock didn't have the effect I wanted. It didn't muffle Brent's words as he muttered, "What the heck? How am I ever going to tell her?"

Whatever he had to say could wait. He apparently didn't care about my feelings.

Chapter Three

Brent

The only good thing about the events of last week was that Kieran, and his Scottish accent, were gone and I could maybe have a chance with Zoe again. Obviously I would take all of my friends being alive and happy over having a chance with Zoe any day, but if there was any silver lining, that had to be it.

Except she was still in love with the jerk, even after everything he'd gone and done. I'd wanted to tell her this morning how I felt and it just fell apart at the mention of Kieran's name. The guy had to be millions of miles away, probably back in Scotland now, and he was still causing problems. How was I ever going to tell her that she didn't need him? That I could love her and would never hurt her the way he had?

My thoughts grew into a jumbled swirl. Sitting outside in the humidity, alone with only my messed up head as company, I decided a swim would clear them. I wasn't wearing swim trunks, but I didn't care. I stripped off my t-shirt and jumped into the water. It was nice and cool compared to the heat in the air and I could almost imagine myself as normal if I treaded water without touching the sides of the pool.

Being able to see through any surface I touch with my hands or feet was a fantastic ability, just overwhelming at times. Learning to control the sense was exhausting. However, the water with its clear liquid felt almost normal. It even seemed to sooth my sore, worn fingertips.

I used to play guitar every day or whenever I had time, but now when I'm alone, I'm almost constantly playing it. The feel of the vibrations of the music through my fingers seems to calm me down and keep me from thinking too much about Zoe, Rylee, or Kieran.

I lay on my back treading water, pretending to play guitar strings in the pool. I'd brought one of my acoustic guitars along and the minute we'd arrived at the villa, I'd double-checked it hadn't been damaged in checkout baggage. I'd practically wrapped the entire thing in bubble wrap but was still worried something might happen to it. I needed it as my form of therapy. I didn't even want to think about what I would have done if it got damaged. It was bad enough I had to live with Zoe while she was still in love with Kieran.

"Good morning," someone called out.

I jumped at the sound of the voice, splashing water. Zoe's dad came out of the sliding doors of the villa with a cup of coffee and a medical journal. He held up a hand in greeting and went to lie down in a hammock that lay adjacent to the pool.

I got out of the pool. "Morning, sir," I said as I tried to shake off the majority of the water droplets dripping off of me before using my shirt to take care of the rest. I dried off as quickly as I could, keeping my back to the man as much as possible. I've been friends with Zoe and her family for years, and her father has seen me shirtless many times from various outings at the beach or just hanging out on a hot day, but ever since that day in the mine, I've been working out with everyone else. I didn't want him asking why I was suddenly buff after years of being the skinny, non-athletic musician. The fact that he was a doctor made it seem like he would notice it even more.

Part of me thinks we should tell Zoe's dad about what happened. He's always been really cool and not the typical kind of parent. Sure, he was Zoe's dad and watched out for her, but he never grilled us on what we were up to or made us feel like most parents did with teenagers. Zoe had told me about him doing blood work on her and Kieran but never came back with results that made him question what might have happened. Maybe nothing showed in our systems. Zoe had mentioned something was high or low or whatever, but he hadn't pushed her or any of us for more bloodwork.

He was a doctor. If we told him, maybe he could find a way to change us back – if we wanted it. Some days the ability felt like a curse but most days I now I couldn't imagine not having it. I grinned. It might come in handy having a doctor around in case any of us got seriously injured in a fight or our new powers start causing serious problems. I waved to him, but he didn't notice, already absorbed in his medical readings. I grinned again as I headed for the villa. That's why he was the perfect guy to take us on holidays. No questions, no demands, no complaints.

I went inside and followed the smell of coffee to the kitchen. I had a feeling Zoe would be all right with telling her dad if I talked it over with her. It was the other two who would be a harder sell, especially Seth. He was still all over it just being our secret and if any outsiders found out, we would be in serious trouble. The big guy read way too many comic books. We weren't superheroes. How could we be of any use to anyone when we can't even keep ourselves from being killed by a stupid car?

"What're you thinking about?" Seth's voice startled me out of my thoughts. "The pensiveness is reeking off of you in waves."

I rolled my eyes. "I thought you could only smell strong emotions." Then I chuckled at him. "That's a big word for you."

"Screw off!" He laughed. "But you're right on the smelling of strong emotions, but you also look pensive and I said your name three times before you responded. It doesn't take a superpower to know you're thinking about something." He took a huge sniff and then walked passed me to grab a cup from the cupboard. "Thank freakin' goodness I like the smell of coffee." He pushed air through his nose. "That smell is going to stay in my nostrils for months."

I sipped my own coffee, glad I didn't have strong smell like Seth or taste like Heidi. I liked junk food and preferred to keep it that way without knowing that the person who cooked my hamburger just got back from a smoke break or was drenched in Axe.

"So what were you thinking?" Seth poured his coffee and added only a dab of milk and sugar. "It looked like whatever it was is bothering you."

"Just stuff." I shrugged. "The usual."

Seth nodded. "Understandable. It's still hard for me too."

I raised an eyebrow. Seth was usually more aggressive and less sympathetic. Maybe he was feeling bad about how he treated Zoe yesterday. If that was the case, then it was her he should be sympathizing with right now, not me. "I know it is. It's hard on all of us." I pushed my eyebrows together determined he would get the point. "That's why you need to go easier on Zoe. She was closer to him than anybody else and she's hurting from it."

"She's still in love with him!" Seth shook his head. "That's why she doesn't want us to go after him. You know it. I know it. Hell, even Heidi knows Zoe's hung up on the Scot, even though Heidi's too cute to ever admit it."

I stayed silent. I couldn't argue with that. "It doesn't matter if she's still emotionally connected to him or not." I'd thought about this a lot. Something else was going on, but I couldn't figure it out. "She was betrayed just as much as the rest of us. Maybe more." I straightened and gave him a hard look. "Unless you think she helped him kill his dad and then Rylee, after committing a string of burglaries with him, even attacking my father."

"Of course not," Seth said quickly. "But her judgment's clouded. I'm not sure we should listen to her idea of just sitting around and letting this murderer go free."

Zoe appeared behind Seth in the doorway. By her look, I knew she had heard every word of it from her room. "And your judgment isn't clouded, Seth?" she growled. "You don't have a personal vendetta because the robbery at Brent's house almost made you lose your best friend? Your judgment isn't clouded by the fact that Rylee, the girl you have been crushing over for years, is dead?"

I looked at Seth, shocked. He had been in love with Rylee? That was news to me. Guess we all had secrets, and skeletons, in the closet.

Seth jumped out of his seat, slamming his coffee mug on the table, the dark liquid splattering everywhere. "I'm not in love with Rylee!" he shouted, cornering Zoe against a wall. "I have never been in love with her. Stop throwing senseless accusations out at everyone who accuses your boyfriend of being guilty of a crime."

"It's not senseless!" Zoe pushed him away from her before I had a chance to step in. Her eyes widened when she looked at his face. "It isn't, is it?"

It had just been a shot in the dark, but it had definitely struck a nerve. Seth looked at her again and stormed out.

Zoe visibly winced with each step. She glared at me. "You wanna go at it, too?"

I shook my head. "I don't think so."

Zoe's dad came rushing in. "What's all of the yelling about? Everyone okay?"

"Nothing." Zoe waved her hand. "Tensions are just high with Seth."

Her father raised an eyebrow. "Is that all?" He stared at her long and hard, even I grew uncomfortable and shifted my weight. "Why do I have the feeling you're not telling me something?"

"It's just a theory," I said before Zoe could reply. "We don't want to spread rumors or cause him more pain."

"Seth?" Zoe's dad asked.

I nodded.

"I understand," he said and sighed. "Try to remember, this is a vacation. Don't dwell on whatever it is too much. The four of you should have some fun." He forced a smile. "Doctor's orders."

Zoe rolled her eyes at her dad's dorkiness.

I grinned as he left and then turned my attention back to Zoe. "Your dad's right, Zoe. This is a vacation. If Seth wants to talk to us, fine. But let's leave it all alone and forget this conversation ever happened until we get back home."

She gave me a shaky smile. "Okay," she said. "I'm for that. If Seth is."

Heidi woke up shortly after and jumped in the pool. After the girls were ready, the five of us went out for lunch at a small restaurant in town. It was a great place, with a view of an old Aztec temple, right outside the window where we sat. A live band played as we ate. I watched them, hypnotized by their music and the way their fingers moved over their instruments. I ached to join them even though I didn't know any of the songs and my guitar was back at the house.

"Do you think we could get a tour of the ruins?" Heidi asked, pulling my attention away from the musicians. "I remember learning about the Aztecs in History class and I'd love to see the temples up close."

"That's a great idea!" Zoe's dad pushed his plate away and leaned back. "At least we can go to some of them. A few are in too poor condition and aren't safe."

Zoe, who had her hands pretty much covering her ears from the live band, dropped them and folded them on her lap. "I'd love to see the ruins, too. The Aztec unit was the most interesting in school."

"Why? Because they ripped the hearts out of the chests of their human sacrifices?" Seth asked.

Zoe made a face. "Well, they did that, but they never killed in battle." She bit her lip as she tried to remember. "They preferred to injure the enemy warriors so they could capture them and use them for sacrifices. You could say they had a healthy respect for life because they thought killing in battle was wasteful."

"I'm sure that mattered so much to their sacrificial victims," Seth joked.

"I have to admit, I'm not into the killing thing. Sounds a bit too gory for me." I finished the last of my fajita. "But the city built on a lake is kind of cool."

"How about we go on a tour tomorrow afternoon?" Zoe's dad asked. "I'll arrange it today." He set his fork down on a plate with a clatter.

Zoe, sitting across from him, winced at the noise.

"Sorry, honey," he said. "I keep forgetting."

You could have heard a pin drop from the silence at our table.

We all looked at Zoe. Was it possible she had told her dad about our powers without talking to us first?

I felt Seth tense up beside me and laid a hand on his arm. Whether or not that was the case, we didn't need a scene at the restaurant.

Zoe's face grew tense as she looked at her dad. "What do you mean, Dad? What do you keep forgetting?"

He looked at his daughter and then at all of us before staring down at his plate. "Nothing." He shrugged.

"Obviously it's not nothing," Seth said in a low, angry voice. "Why don't you just tell us?"

He looked at all of our tense faces and forced a smile. "The rest of you must've noticed she can now hear exceptionally well." He looked at his daughter. "She once answered me when I said her name from down the hall under my breath."

Zoe flushed. "You were louder than you thought," she muttered.

"No, I really wasn't." He looked at the rest of us, the excitement plain on his face. "The rest of you must've noticed." He waited a heartbeat of a second before continuing. "And you would all think it reasonable if you had similar abilities, wouldn't you? Did the same thing happen to the rest of you that happened to Zoe in the mine?"

Seth crossed his arms. "I have no idea what you're talking about." He glared at Zoe. "There's nothing wrong or unusual about us."

"Wait," I blurted out. The others looked at me, surprised. "He's already figured it out," I told them. "We might as well tell him."

"I still don't know what you're talking about," Seth growled, now glaring at me. "Everyone, zip it."

"No, Seth." I turned to Zoe's dad, meeting his gaze head on. "He's not going to tell anyone, is he? That's why he brought us here."

"Of course, not," Zoe's dad said, taking a sip of his lemonade. "Actually, I wouldn't be able to legally if all of you became my patients. There is doctor-patient confidentiality after all." He couldn't stop the corner of his lips from raising.

"Fine." I grinned back, liking Zoe's dad even more. "That solves it."

"No, it doesn't—"

"Shut up, Seth."

"All of us got superpowers when we were in the mine," Heidi blurted out.

Chapter Four

Zoe

I stared at my dad, unable to figure him out. He'd known? On top of that, he'd tested me to see if it was true? He had my bloodwork and Kieran's. How long had he known? "I can't believe you tricked me." I should have been mad at him. Instead, all I felt was relief. Like a weight had been lifted off my shoulders. "Why didn't you tell me you knew?"

He had the decency to look embarrassed. "I hoped you'd tell me in your own time." He put on his unreadable doctor's face. "If it weren't for that slip of my tongue, none of you would have known I already knew."

"You knew about *all* of us?" Seth accused.

I could feel his glare on me and I couldn't even look at him. He had no right to be angry at me. How was I supposed to know Dad figured it out? I hadn't done anything wrong.

"I had my theories," Dad explained, using his hands to gesture as he talked. "However, when Kieran's blood results came back normal, I did consider the possibility that it was only Zoe who had been affected. It just didn't make sense, though. The trace uranium in that room and the electricity from the lightning, it," he hesitated and glanced at me a second before continuing, "It should have riddled your body with complications."

I bit my lip. I never did tell Dad that Kieran had switched the blood test results. He still didn't know Kieran also had superpowers. It was for the best he didn't know. I didn't need him worrying about our safety from my psychic boyfriend. *Ex-*

boyfriend, Zoe. How did he switch the blood results anyway? He would have had to have gotten past Dad's nurse, probably. Unless he broke in at night like he did all of the other break-ins. I winced at the thought. That was probably exactly what he had done.

"What do you mean riddled with complications?" Seth stopped accusing as his tone turned to one of worry.

Heidi hit his arm. "He means cancer or our organs shutting down. We are all fine, Seth. Nothing's changed for the worse."

I stared at Heidi in surprise. She sounded like the old Heidi, and yet stronger.

"We all can't hear like Zoe." Brent crossed his arms over his chest and hid his hands under his armpits. "This isn't exactly the place we should be having this conversation."

No one argued. We didn't stay much longer at the restaurant and headed back to the house in a tense silence. Despite the fact that this was supposed to be a vacation, no one was really in the mood to forget about reality. Especially the reality of our superpower senses.

I tuned out Dad's quiet conversation with Brent as Heidi and Seth chatted in front of me as we walked back to the villa. Instead, I took in the sounds of the small town with children playing and the wind blowing. I heard all of their heartbeats mixed with the sounds of running feet, moving cars, and people talking to create a strange song that made up the essence of life. *It's a shame Brent didn't get this power. He would be able to appreciate it much more than I can.* It didn't help that I was slightly jealous of Brent's power. Aside from thinking too much about where he could put his hands and the awkwardness with him touching my or Heidi's shirt, he had it pretty good. No headaches like me, or nausea like Seth and Heidi.

The floating conversations in Spanish were nice to listen to. The language sounded almost musical when spoken by native speakers, unlike the Spanish teacher at school or my classmates who stumbled over the pronunciation without bothering to pick up the accent no matter how much the teacher begged. The words just rolled off the tongues of the natives.

"*Discúlpeme, senor,*" someone said and I gasped, coming to a halt.

Brent walked into me from behind. "Keep moving, Zoe." His warm fingers pressed against my bare shoulders. "Everything all right?"

I stared at him while concentrating on a conversation who knew how far away. The person who had spoken was definitely not a native.

"You're not from 'ere, *senor,*" an older man said in broken English. "Britain?"

"Scotland, actually," came the reply. "I'm here to surprise a friend."

The old Spanish man chuckled. "Why aren't you with her right now?"

"We didn't part on the best of terms and I'm a tad nervous." Kieran hesitated. "How did you know it was a 'her'."

The other man laughed. "When you get to be my age, young man, you can just tell these things."

I blocked the rest of the conversation and pushed the balls of my feet against the concrete as I sprinted into a run back home. I heard Brent call for me, but I ignored it.

I ran straight around to the back of the villa and jumped fully clothed into the pool. Sitting at the bottom of the shallow end, I absorbed the silence and tried to organize my chaotic thoughts.

So Kieran was in Mexico. He knew I was here and had followed me. The thought filled me with dread. The others would be angry. Seth would tear him apart with his bare hands.

Yet, I wanted so badly to see him. To press my hand against his, feel his lips brush against mine. Stare into those unbelievable green eyes. I blew bubbles and watched them float to the top of the water. I still wanted to see him, to have him pull me into his arms and say it was going to be okay. Have him wake me from this dream and Rylee would still be alive and he would be innocent.

I pushed my knees against the bottom of the pool and stood up, forcing fresh, clean air filled with oxygen into my lungs. I knew that wasn't going to happen. Rylee was dead and Kieran was the one who caused it whether he meant to or not.

He'd murdered his father and then tried to cover it up. He'd only been acting out of self-defence but running away from the law had ruined any fair chance he'd ever get.

I walked to the side of the pool and pulled myself up, letting my feet, sneakers included, hang in the water.

"Zoe, is everything okay?" Brent put his hand on my shoulder and I jumped.

"Sorry," I said, smiling weakly at him. "Just suddenly felt like I needed a moment on my own."

"You took off like a swarm of bees was after you."

I nodded. It didn't seem like he was too far off.

Chapter Five

I couldn't tell anyone that Kieran was in Mexico.

Things were still simmering from us admitting to Dad about what happened because of the night in the mine. Even though Seth didn't believe it, Dad wasn't going to tell anyone. Seth stormed to his room and Heidi and Brent followed after him to try and convince him it would be handy having an adult on our side and a doctor to boot. I agreed with them and pretended I needed to have a rest. Neither argued with me as I headed to my room and lay on the bed staring up at the ceiling.

How had he found us? How could he travel without alerting the police? Could he be here to hurt me? Or did he want to talk?

I wanted Kieran to be innocent, I really did. The fact he was here tracking me down must mean he really did care about me. Perhaps not all of it had been an act after all. *It didn't matter. Not after what he did.* I knew he was trouble. He killed his father out of self-defence, but Rylee... A tear slid down from my eye and teased my ear. It didn't matter what he felt for me because it didn't change what had happened. He should have just gone to the police and confessed. That's what he *would* have done if he had not intended to kill anybody. I groaned as I rolled over and buried my face in my pillow, silently screaming.

There was a knock on my door, and the sound of a heavy heartbeat that was faster and less healthy than that of any of my friends. Ever since we started working out, our resting heart rates had slowed dramatically. This beat was familiar but not one of ours. "Dad?" I called out.

"Zoe-zey, can I come in?"

I sat up. "Sure." Now that he openly admitted he knew, she imagined him asking for more bloodwork or maybe he wanted to talk about what my powers might mean scientifically. I clenched my jaw. I just wasn't in the mood.

He came in and I made room for him to sit on the bed. He awkwardly perched on the side. His brow was furrowed in concern. "I didn't mean to cause conflict between you and your friends. I wish I hadn't said anything at all."

"It's okay." I sighed. "Seth'll come around. He always does."

"That's not all that's bothering you, is it?"

I hesitated only for a moment before shaking my head. "Dad... what did you think of Kieran when you met him?"

He stared at me for a long time. "Kieran is what's bothering you?"

I nodded. He didn't get it. "I just... The whole thing is very confusing." *That's the understatement of the year.* "It's really hard to put together what I know, and what I think I know about him." *Or try and figure out what information goes in which category.* "Does that even make sense?"

Her dad patted her knee. "Well, I only met him the one time, but he seemed perfectly nice and normal when I did. Very laidback and liking you very much. I would have to say that it's very hard to see him as a killer." He shrugged. "I don't know. It seems to me... if he was able to lie about his father being in Scotland for so long, then I'm sure there is more to him than meets the eye. He could hide more than either you or I know. I'm sure not all of it is good."

I sighed. "But he was so sweet," I whispered. "I was thinking, maybe he didn't mean to hurt Rylee. The weather was really bad that night. Maybe it obstructed his vision, or maybe an animal or something jumped into the road and swerved." I was crying, I sounded desperate but I didn't care.

"Perhaps," Dad said. "But if that was the case, then why didn't he go to the police? I know you want to believe the best in him,

Zoe-zey. Believe me, I'm the same way. I want to always see the best in the people I love as well. However, we both know it's not always the case. Sometimes it isn't meant to be."

I knew he was thinking about Mom. He never started dating again after they had split up and he still wore his wedding ring when he was at home. Impulsively, I reached out and hugged him as if I was a little girl again. "I know, Dad. It's just me wishing. Thank you for talking with me."

He smiled and ruffled my hair. "Anytime, Zoe-zey. This is all part of a healing process, of letting go. It's good to talk. I'm always here for you, sweetie. Always." He hugged me again.

"I'm okay, Dad." I wiped my face. "I'm glad you know."

"Me, too."

"How long did you know?"

"For a while. I don't know about the others and their symptoms but I would love to find out. We could do some bloodwork and run some tests. It'll be harder without my lab, but there's so much to learn—"

I stood and cut him off, "I think I'll go for a swim."

He stared, his mouth still open and his eyes still forming ideas on what he wanted to do. He inhaled a sharp breath and then slowly released it. "Okay then, I'm going to go make a few calls and see if we can take a tour of some of the ruins. Maybe you guys can even get some extra credit in history class if you do."

I wrinkled my nose. "Let's not spoil the vacation."

He laughed and left the room.

I sighed. It was tempting to just curl up into a ball and mope again. Even though it was nice having a conversation with my dad about things, I wasn't any closer than I was before to having my feelings sorted out. "Kieran, who are you?" I whispered.

Chapter Six

Kieran

"Ya killed her!" my father screamed. "It was ya! I know it was!" He hit me again with his bloodied knuckles, and another whiff of Scotch and sweat hurled past me. I curled my lip in distaste.

"Da," I begged. "It's me, your son. Please stop."

"You killed her, you son of a whore. I know who ya damn ah." He grabbed the whisky bottle off the table and drank the rest of it before raising it over his head.

I stared in horror at him. In that instant I knew he was going to kill me.

I woke gasping, drenched in sweat that had nothing to do with the heat. I curled into the fetal position, breathing hard and trying to calm my racing heart. That was the third nightmare this week, and the worse one yet. I had been having them ever since the day with my dad, when he dragged me out to the mine. I shuddered at the thought of it. Since Rylee's death, they had only gotten worse. *At least Zoe isn't in any of them. Yet.*

No, Zoe haunted me during the day. The fear and horror that crossed her face when she believed what had happened... it made me sick to my stomach.

There was a knock on the motel room door. "Senor?" a timid female voice called out. "Are you all right? There have been complaints about screaming coming from here." Her English was broken and heavily accented, but I could sense the meaning of her words as well as if she was a native English speaker. I also knew what she looked like. I could sense it as well. She was young, probably only a teenager herself, very thin and pretty with curly black hair and eyes the color of chocolate. I could also feel her nervousness. She was probably new or the daughter of the owner, sent to do his dirty work.

"I'm all right," I called. "Sorry for the disturbance."

"Okay. Senor."

I listened to her footsteps as she went away and then sat back down, feeling a headache coming on. My sixth sense was killing me. I still didn't know exactly what I had. I referred to it as my sixth sense, a heightened ability like the other five. I swallowed. Four now. I sighed and rubbed my temple with my thumbs. Sometimes it felt like I could see the future, other times it felt like I could read people's minds. But not well. Otherwise I wouldn't have messed up so badly with Zoe.

Instead of going back to sleep and enduring another nightmare, I turned on the light and pulled my suitcase out from under my bed. As long as I was awake, I might as well be working.

Chapter Seven

Zoe

The Aztec ruins were made of crumbling beige stone and winding trails throughout different remains of the buildings. They were beautiful and sad all at once. I liked exploring them. Heidi was happy; grinning, taking pictures from every angle, and Seth too was smiling as he ran his hand over the stones while reading the information on the plaques. He had been miserable and cranky when we woke and over breakfast Brent went through the advantages of have a doctor know, be willing to keep our secret, and help us. His bad mood couldn't stay when the strongest scent he had was fresh air and earth.

"It's pretty wild, isn't it?" Brent asked.

"I love it!" I turned around and enjoyed the full panoramic view. "It's so pretty."

He grinned. "It's perfect." He pointed to a flat top of one of the temples. "That would be an excellent place to play the guitar. Don't you think? Maybe circle of friends at the top with me, or screaming crowd below."

"I'm pretty sure that's where they sacrificed their victims to their gods. You sure that's where you want to play guitar?" I couldn't help but giggle.

He shrugged, trying to keep a straight face. "You're right. Best not to disrespect other people's religion."

I grinned. "Yeah, *that's* the reason you don't want to play guitar there."

"Hey, it's part of it. I'm not Mel Gibson."

I left the others who wanted to see a ruin up a steep hill, electing to rest and enjoy the hot sun. Brent looked like he wanted to argue but, thankfully, my dad pulled him along. I sat down on the ground on the edge of the main road. With my eyes closed and the breeze on my face, I opened myself up to the sounds of the wind, different animals crawling in the grass, and tourists chattering as they roamed through the ruins. Beyond that was the sound of the modern civilization in the distance, with cars on the road and a cell phone ringing on high volume in the nearby village.

"Zoe."

I gasped and scrambled to my feet. I stared at the dusty, dirt ground below. *Kieran.* "What're you doing here?"

I heard his heartbeat increase. "No, don't run away," he pleaded. "Please. I'd never hurt you, Zoe. You have to believe me."

I heard the sincerity in his voice. I was backing away from him and I made myself stay still. "What're you doing here?" I repeated, in a whisper this time.

"I only came here to see you for a few minutes." He looked desperate. His dark hair had grown and now fell over his beautiful blue eyes.

"What do you want, Kieran?" His name escaped my lips and suddenly I wished his mouth was on mine.

He pressed his lips together before smiling, as if he'd read my thoughts. "I didn't know you meditated."

"I-It's part of our t-training," I stuttered, nervously babbling and happy about the change of subject. "It's not really meditation." I looked over my shoulder to where the rest of the group had gone. "The others—"

"Screw them," he whispered fiercely. "I have no intention of seeing them, or vice versa. They have no idea I'm here. I've figured a way to disguise myself." He stepped closer and I caught a whiff of strong perfume.

I almost laughed. "I guess you did. Not even Seth could smell you under that stench. I'm sure Heidi has a mouthful of chemicals right now."

He grimaced. "I can't stay long." He glanced toward where the others had disappeared, as if expecting them to appear any moment. "I followed you here. I couldn't help it."

"Why?" *Because I'm a psychopath?* I shook my head to clear my inner thought. Somehow, deep inside me, I wanted to give him a chance. I knew he was guilty, I just couldn't stop thinking he was a victim.

"I came because I had to tell you I didn't kill Rylee, okay?" He ran his fingers through his hair, his blue eyes shining bright. "I wouldn't, I'd never hurt any of you."

"How am I supposed—" I let my voice trail off as he turned and raced away, disappearing as he dove behind a wall.

"Zoe!" Brent called from behind me.

I jerked, his voice sounding like he was right behind me, yelling in my ear. I turned slowly, expecting him there.

He was up on a set of old limestone stairs. "Come on! You're missing some really good sights."

I turned and ran to catch up to him, refusing to look back if Kieran might still be behind me. His arrival only meant trouble.

Brent's expression turned to one of concern as he stared at me. "What's wrong?"

I forced a smile and forced myself not to look over my shoulder. "Nothing," I lied. "Guess I didn't want to be on my own." I put my hand over my eyes to see the view behind Brent. "Wow! You're right. These are some really good sights."

Both Seth and Heidi gagged when we caught up to them.

"Holy shit, Zoe!" Seth plugged his nose. "Where in the world did you find that perfume? It's horrendous."

Heidi covered her mouth and then mumbled something at me from behind her hand. I couldn't tell exactly what she was saying, but the sentiment was similar to Seth's.

"There were a couple of teenage girls spraying each other back there." I fanned myself. "I tried to get away from it. I didn't realize they'd hit me as well." Kieran had been right; Seth and Heidi couldn't detect him from under the perfume.

Dad watched us in fascination. "I really would like to perform some tests on you guys." He waved his hands, realizing he probably sounded like a mad scientist. "Just to see what you guys can do. Nothing crazy."

"How about we talk about it when we get back home, okay, Doc?" Brent wiped his forehead from the heat. "We're on vacation right now.'"

We headed up the long stairs to the ruins. My mind couldn't stop picturing Kieran or thinking about what he had said. *I didn't kill Rylee. I would never hurt any of you.* Hope welled up inside of me.

Chapter Eight

Brent

"You okay?" I asked Zoe. "You seem quiet."

"Huh? Oh, I'm fine. Just a little tired. The engines are giving me a headache."

I knew the plane was giving her a headache, just like it was making Seth and Heidi incapacitated with nausea. However, she had been quiet for most of our time in Mexico. Something was different about her, but I couldn't put my finger on it. Ever since the ruins tour she'd grown quiet. She might just be missing Kieran. Or finally accepting he was guilty.

I didn't know myself whether Kieran was guilty or not, but a selfish part of me really hoped he was. I knew he was, but exactly of what drove me crazy. I couldn't figure it out. If he was guilty then there would be a legitimate reason to keep him away from Zoe, and not just because I was in love with her, but every time I thought about it, it didn't really add up. He didn't drive a car, and Rylee was definitely hit by a car. Kieran drove a motorbike. There were two sets of tracks in the snow that night and he was on his bike. He could have hit her and then driven away making the two tracks. It just seemed wishful thinking on my part.

Plus, he would have known that if he killed one of us, he would have to kill all of us to keep his secret. So why kill one and then just run? But if he was innocent, why didn't he go to the police when his father went missing? And why did he break into all of those places? For money?

The only person who could answer those questions was unfortunately the last person I ever wanted to see again.

Zoe sighed beside me. "I wish we didn't have to go back. Reality seems to suck these days."

"Believe me, I don't either," I said. "We do have to go to school. Going to Mexico during a vacation is one thing. Going there when school is starting is another. I don't want to spend any more time in high school than necessary."

Zoe made a face. "I know, but it's cold up there. I feel cold up there."

I knew she wasn't just talking about the temperature. The bad memories in Elliot Lake haunted us and made the mood gloomy even on warm sunny days. They gave chills to all of us. I know I rarely felt warm up there as well. "It's going to be okay." I reached for her hand and then let mine drop before touching hers. "It will get warmer. I promise. If not, we can take off to university soon."

She shook her head and then leaned her head on my shoulder, closing her eyes. "Hey, Brent?" she mumbled.

I swallowed, wishing we could stay like this forever. "Yeah, Zoe?"

"Do you think Dad will find a way to get rid of our powers?"

I looked down at her and realized she was completely serious. "Becoming normal again won't bring Rylee back, Zoe. Life won't return to normal just because your hearing does."

She was quiet a moment. "I know. Maybe it'll keep us from getting killed." She inhaled a long slow breath before slowly letting it out. "I don't want to play superhero anymore. We were stupid to think we could."

"None of us are going to die. We're smarter, now. We'll be on our guard. Kieran's not coming back for us. He won't do that."

"Being smart isn't enough. We were careful and look what happened to Rylee."

"We weren't careful enough," I whispered. "Besides, Kieran's gone now. No one else here is going to betray us."

Zoe hesitated before saying quietly, so only I would hear, "I don't think Kieran did it."

"He did," I said a little too vehemently, a little too loud. "There's no other explanation for it. He killed his father, and when Rylee found out, he killed her too."

"How does that even make any sense?" She pulled away from me. "Think about it, Brent. He didn't kill Rylee."

"He's not innocent, Zoe." I couldn't believe we were having this conversation. "He knew something had happened to his father, didn't he?"

She hesitated for a second, looking down at her hands. "I don't know about his father," she said finally, "but there's no way he killed Rylee."

I could see she had just as much proof for his innocence as I did for his guilt. When she looked at me, I knew she needed to believe he wasn't the one who killed Rylee. If he was, then she had lost her boyfriend forever as well as one of her closest friends, and she couldn't deal with that. I sighed. "He might be innocent," I said finally. "We'll let the police do their work and find him and solve the case. If we can, we'll help them."

Zoe shook her head. "I'm not helping them. Especially not for the murder of Kieran's father. Not in any role except that of a civilian."

The hatred in her voice made me think it wasn't just helping Kieran that made her so against solving the murder. "You met Kieran's father before, didn't you? What was he like?"

Zoe glared at me before turning in her seat to face the window, putting her headphones on, effectively ending the conversation. I faced forward and tried to read the magazine I had brought for the plane trip. Unfortunately, it was too hot to wear gloves and my hands kept touching the page so I could see my blue jeans behind the words on the page. After a while of trying to focus on the words and not whatever was behind gave me a headache so I put the magazine away.

"Hey," Seth said, tapping my arm. "What's with Zoe? She okay?"

I glanced at Zoe, knowing full well she could hear every word we were saying, even if she did crank her white noise app up to the highest volume. "She's fine." I pointed to my head. "Just has a headache."

"When we get back, we're totally going to go back up to the mines." Seth rubbed his hands together. "That's the last spot any of us saw Kieran. There might be clues up there that can help us track him down."

I nodded absently. Maybe Zoe was right about Seth having a thing for Rylee. He had turned even more revenge-set than the rest of us after Rylee's death. I had a feeling it was blurring what little judgement he had. "We'll talk about it when we get back, okay? The police have already been up there, and they haven't found anything, have they?"

"The police are just civilians with badges," Seth said. "They don't have powers like we do."

"What're you going to do, smell the ground?" I snapped. "Do you want me to see if he conveniently stashed a love letter to Zoe in a tree trunk that has his new address stamped on it? The police might not have superpowers, but they do have teams of people trained to solve crimes and find clues. What the hell are we supposed to do? Besides, I would like to remind you that we are not immortal."

Anger ignited in Seth's eyes and just as he was about to fire a retort, Heidi sat forward suddenly. "Guys," she hissed. "People are watching us. Right now. Seth, switch places with me and both of you calm the hell down. I can taste the testosterone between the two of you."

Seth's lip curled in disgust but he did switch places with Heidi, who gave me a reassuring smile. "It's going to be all right," she murmured. "We'll figure out what we should do after we get back to Elliot Lake. Not a moment before."

She was turning into the responsible one taking care of all of us. She always had been in a way, but now she was even more so. I pretended to sleep the rest of the flight and ignored everyone.

As soon as the plane landed, Zoe stormed off as quickly as she could, ignoring our calls to come back.

Her dad looked in the direction she went. "I'll talk to her. I'm not sure how much good it can do, but coming home is going to be hard on all of you." He went off to follow his daughter.

We just watched him go and stood waiting for our luggage. I was torn at following Zoe or giving her space.

"Let's all meet at Brent's in one hour," Seth said. "Without Zoe."

"Why without her?" Heidi asked.

"She dated Kieran and she's clearly still hung up on him. I bet she's still in contact with him all this time and feeding him information to keep him out of harm's way." Comic book guy's mind had been running rampant. "I think it's best we watch what we say in front of her until we know she can be trusted."

"You're being ridiculous, Seth," I growled. "We grew up with Zoe. There's no way she's not trust-worthy."

"We thought Kieran was trustworthy." Seth threw his bag over his back. "Look how that turned out. We thought Elliot Lake was a safe place with very little crime and where no one dies of anything short of old age. Look how that turned out, Brent. We don't know anything anymore and we had better start acting like it."

I shook my head. "You're insane. I know what we thought and what happened. I'm not going to walk around paranoid all the time. That's no way to live."

"For people like us, that's the only way to live." Seth stared at me and then stalked off. Heidi reluctantly followed, probably to try and calm him down. With both of them gone, I was left standing alone, more sure than ever that Zoe had a point about our powers.

I had driven Seth and Heidi to the airport and waited to see if they needed a ride back. When I sent Heidi a text, she replied that Seth's mom was coming to get them. I didn't argue. The time alone seemed easier than arguing with them. I called out when I unlocked the front door to my house. No one was home. It didn't really surprise me, even though I had been gone for a week. Both of my parents were probably working or at some social event. Or maybe they were home and just didn't hear me come in. We did live in a mansion, after all. It wouldn't be the first time one of us didn't hear someone come in the house.

Of course, a big house had its pros and cons. There wasn't always someone disturbing you accidentally by going outside while you were doing your homework, but you also didn't hear when a complete stranger came in the house. Unfortunately, Kieran took advantage of that and surprised my dad in his office one day, robbing him blind. At least, I think it was Kieran. My dad refused to talk about who had assaulted him that day, not to mention why he had so much cash on him to begin with.

"I'm home!" I shouted, feeling a little stupid as I went up to my room. I had just come back to Elliot Lake only twenty minutes ago and I was already ready to leave. I wasn't sure if it was because of the sour memories here or because of Seth's most recent insanity. He had always been a jackass, but calling Zoe a traitor was a new low. She was just as much friends with Rylee as all of us. She wouldn't do anything to hurt her, even if they had been competing for the same guy. "Stupid fucking Kieran," I muttered as I went to my room. How the hell would I ever compete for Zoe's heart with that smooth-talking Scot? I couldn't. That was it. He had everything I lacked. He was cool, confident, good-looking to the ladies, foreign. I had money, and a guitar collection. Real exciting. Shit.

I opened my guitar case and began strumming. Playing always relieved stress for me and put me in a better mood. At least, it usually did. Not today. As I played "Greensleeves" from memory, my cell buzzed in my pocket. I set the guitar carefully down on my bed and answered it. Caller ID showed Heidi. "Hello?"

"Hey, it's me," she said. "Can I come up?"

"Of course. Is it already time for the meeting?" I checked my watch. Only fifteen minutes had passed.

"No, but can I come in anyway? I'm sorry, but the front door's locked."

"I'll be right down." I put my guitar away. Heidi never came over on her own. We never hung out much unless we were with everyone. In fact, she usually hung out with people in a group setting unless she was with Zoe and sometimes Rylee. She had always struck me as incredibly shy and more comfortable alone than with people.

Heidi did not look calm when I opened the door. If her chewing on her lip with her arms tightly crossed was any indication. "Come in," I said, moving aside for her to come in. "What's going on?"

"I'm worried about Seth. He's really upset." She scurried in and stood, arms crossed over her chest, hugging herself tight.

"Rylee's death hit him hard." I remembered he was also the first of us to become friends with Kieran. "He feels responsible for it as well."

"He does." Heidi nodded. "He was also in love with her. Can we sit down?"

"Let's go up to my room." I turned and headed for the stairs. "How do you know this?"

Heidi shrugged. "It's really just a hunch, but I'm often right on my hunches. I don't know why, but I'm good at observation."

"Probably because you rarely talk. Much." I grinned.

She bit her lip. "Is it that obvious? I thought I was okay in group things."

"It's only obvious if you think about it," I said quickly. "And there's nothing wrong with being quiet. Sometimes I wished more people were quieter instead of being in love with the sound of their own voices."

She gave me a small smile. "I'm glad you don't care."

I looked at her, trying to figure out what she meant.

Up in my room, she plopped down on the bed, where I quickly moved the guitar out of harm's way. I sat down across from her. Oddly, I wondered why I had suggested my room and now we were sitting on my bed. No parents. No distraction. Heidi was crazy pretty. Any guy would be lucky to be in my situation right now.

"I'm worried about Seth."

And poof! There went the girl in my bedroom appeal. "You think he was in love with Rylee?"

"Half of his obnoxious personality was because he wanted to impress her. She never gave him the time of day because she was always chasing whatever new boy, or older guy, looked at her."

"Really?" I didn't believe her gut feeling. Seth flirted with anything in a skirt. This was grade school talk. "If he was being obnoxious to impress her, then why is he more of an asshole than ever?"

"Because he's angry and he's grieving and he doesn't know how to deal with it because he never told anyone that he had a crush on her. He doesn't want to admit it now."

My brow furrowed. "How the hell do you know all of this?"

She smiled. "I don't own a smartphone, I need something else to do to entertain myself."

"How accurate are your hunches?"

"You tell me," she said. "You like Zoe. Why don't you tell her?"

I flushed. "We've been friends for years, I wouldn't spend time with her if I didn't like her."

"That's not what I meant and you know it," Heidi said, her tone completely serious. "I've seen the way you look at her, especially after she started showing an interest in Kieran. I'm also pretty sure you almost told her and you stopped yourself just in time."

I sighed. "You are way too observant." I was pooched. She would tell Zoe and then any chance of ever having anything was gone. "Why are you telling me all this? To make me feel like shit?"

"Because you're one of the least biased persons here." Heidi folded her hands in her lap. "I mean, we're all upset over Rylee's death and Kieran's betrayal. But Zoe was dating him and Seth was in love with Rylee and good friends with Kieran. You're in love with Zoe, but you're nice enough not to hold her affection for Kieran against her or Kieran. Then there's me. I'm friends with everyone but not particularly close with anyone. Dr. Landers is probably the least biased because he wasn't even in the mine with us. He doesn't even really know about the drama. I'm worried about Seth. I think he's going to do something stupid."

"Not much different than every other day." The joke didn't have the effect on Heidi that I had meant. "What do you think he's going to do?" I had a good idea what he was planning.

"I don't think he's going to let the authorities take care of this one. Brent, I can't stop him alone, but I don't want him to go to jail for murder. That's what I'm worried about."

My mouth went dry. I knew Seth's judgement was clouded. He was angry at himself and Kieran and he could be an asshole a lot of the time. But a murderer? It was hard to tell at this point. It was hard to judge anything at this point. Everything just had to keep getting more complicated. "I'll watch him. Seth and I have been friends since preschool."

"If anyone can stop him, it's you."

"Don't worry, Heidi. I'll make sure he doesn't do anything stupid."

She smiled. "Thank you. I'm glad. I don't want anything else to happen to the group, you know?"

"I getchya." Suddenly, I had a hunch of my own and I understood what she meant about not hiding behind electronics. "Heidi? Don't take this the wrong way, because I really mean no offense, but do you like Seth?"

She blushed but then she smiled at me. "That's none of your business." She stood and turned toward the door. "I'm going down to the gym, if that's okay."

"Need a little stress relieving before our meeting?"

She nodded.

Dad had forbidden us from using the gym after he saw that it was all rearranged, but he had been pretty lax on the rules since Rylee's death. Besides, he wasn't home, might not be home for a while, and never went into the gym anyway. "Go for it."

She waved at me and then left, leaving me alone in my room with my guitar. A tapping on the window made me jump. I glanced over and rushed to open the window when I noticed Zoe hanging off of the branches of a tree near my bedroom. "What are you doing?" I hissed. "You're going to hurt yourself."

"I have excellent balance now, remember?" Zoe laughed. "Things that were dangerous before aren't anymore."

"You said yourself you want to get rid of your powers, so why get used to them now?"

She made a face. "Look," she said, crawling through the window and sitting on my bed. "I'm not working with Kieran and I'm tired of being accused of that by Seth."

Of course she had heard everything. For someone so obsessed with our super senses, he forgot easily about everyone else's. "I don't think you would ever betray us, Zoe. Seth's judgement is clouded. Heidi actually came here because she's worried Seth is going to become dangerous." I hesitated, suddenly wondering if she'd heard the conversation between Heidi and I. Or how much had she heard? I swallowed, unable to look her in the face.

"I know," she said finally. "I heard. I'm not sure it's Seth Heidi likes, by the way." She raised an eyebrow at me.

I shrugged. If she wasn't going to mention my feelings for her, then neither was I. "I've never been good at reading people. Except you. Sometimes. I know you're hiding something from me even though I know you're not betraying us."

"I'm not, really." She bit her lip. "I do miss Kieran, okay? And I think he didn't kill Rylee."

I walked over to the door and checked to make sure it was locked at the same time I used my hand to check the hallway through the door. Nobody was about and all seemed quiet. Heidi was probably beating the shit out of a heavy bag in the gym and Seth hadn't arrived yet.

I went over and sat down next to Zoe. "You know," I said quietly, "you keep saying he didn't kill Rylee, but I'm not sure if I've ever once heard you say he didn't kill his father."

Zoe suddenly couldn't look me in the eye. She seemed more interested in a spec of fluff on the duvet than talking. She was definitely hiding something about Kieran's dad. Either Kieran had told her something, or she had figured it out herself, but she knew something. "It's not really my place to say. Kieran didn't even want me to know."

I wanted to shake her. Why was she giving him the benefit of the doubt? He was guilty. "You can tell me. I promise I won't tell anyone else, not even Heidi or your dad. Certainly not Seth. You know how Seth can be sometimes. It'll just make him want to kill Kieran more." I hated the fact that he had stolen Zoe before I even really had a chance to make her think of me as anything but a friend. But aside from that, I wanted him to be innocent. He seemed like a cool guy. I wanted Zoe to be happy, even if it wasn't with me. If Zoe believed him to be innocent of Rylee's death, then somebody needed to help him.

Her words came out hesitantly. "Kieran's dad was abusive. Not just verbally. I saw the bruises even when Kieran tried to brush them off. His dad was a drunk who couldn't hold down a job and he beat Kieran. He blamed Kieran for his mother's death!

She had cancer and his dad was in the military. He was gone and when he came back, he blamed Kieran. He was brutal!" Her face grew red as she got angry. "Kieran told me what happened to his dad. The night he died, do you know what he did? He forced Kieran in the trunk of his car and drove up to the mine in a drunken rage! Kieran thought he was going to kill him! It was self-defence!"

"He just told you that? Out of the blue?" Maybe Kieran was trying to score points of sympathy with Zoe. I knew I was only trying to fool myself.

"I met his dad. He was drunk! He spoke to Kieran like he was nothing but garbage! His dad put a lock on Kieran's door so he couldn't get out. He would force him into his room and who knows what else he had to endure!" She wiped her eyes with the back of her hand. "It's not fair. He didn't deserve that."

I understood her pity, could even sympathize with it. However, the fact that he never reported his father missing stopped me from believing Kieran was completely innocent. If what Zoe was saying was true, then Kieran might have not killed intentionally at all. It could be self-defence. He could have buried his dad in a panic. "When did you meet his father?"

"Only once," Zoe said. "Kieran tried to keep me away from him. He didn't know his dad was home. He wanted me to wait in the car but I heard him and Kieran fighting. His father did threaten to beat him up and then later that night, when all of us were together, he came in bruised."

I sat back, trying to process this information. Kieran's father was an abusive drunk. So Kieran could have killed him out of self-defence. I could hear the sincerity in Zoe's words and I knew she believed them to be true. "It doesn't explain why he covered up the body and tried to hide it. I mean, wouldn't it have been smarter just to go to the police and tell them what happened? There's no way he would have been convicted for defending himself."

"Maybe the law works differently in Scotland." Zoe gestured with her hands. "Perhaps he was scared of being sent to jail. He panicked. Maybe his dad said if Kieran ever reported him, he would only cause trouble. Maybe it was better when his dad was gone. Maybe that was the best time of his life. I'm not sure if he has anyone left over in Scotland. Besides..." She trailed off and bit her lip, looking down at her lap. "I'm here," she whispered. She hugged her knees to her chest and shifted slightly over. "Sorry," she said as tears ran down her face. "I have to say it. There's a good chance that he actually cares enough about me to cover up a killing."

"Why would you—Ohhh." I closed my eyes and groaned. "You heard the entire conversation between Heidi and me, didn't you?"

She nodded. "I didn't mean to eavesdrop, really. But it was kind of hard not to after a while." She smiled at me, looking beautiful with the tears on her face. "Why didn't you tell me, Brent?"

"I wasn't sure for a long time," I mumbled. "And then I was too nervous because I didn't want to make things awkward between us, and you were starting to like Kieran, so it wasn't really my place, was it?"

She wrapped her arms around my waist. "Well, I'm glad I know. I wish I knew earlier, though."

"Really?"

"Yes," she said, looking up at me. She bit her lip in that cute way that made my entire body go warm. "I'd have said yes to a date if you had asked."

"Damn," I swore. I smiled ruefully at her. There was still a chance. Maybe not right at this moment, but I was pretty sure I'd wait forever for her. "Well, should have, would have, could have, huh?"

"I guess so. You mean a lot to me, Brent. I can't imagine my life without you in it." She sat up and kissed me on the cheek. "You're an amazing friend, Brent. Really."

"Except now there's Kieran. You honestly think I want him in jail because he's dating you?" Well, I did a little. But not enough to actually put him there. "I want you to be happy, Zoe. If Kieran makes you happy... I have to be okay with that."

"I know, but..."

I put my arm around her and pulled her even closer to me. "No buts. Let's prove he's not guilty and then move forward from there. Who knows, I might get you to fall in love with me along the way. Or maybe not." I laughed. "I'm only messing, gorgeous!"

Zoe leaned her head against my shoulder, lost in thought. I tensed as she did it. We had sat like this many times over the years for various reasons. Especially after Rylee's death. Now it felt different because she knew about my feelings for her. She seemed perfectly relaxed, but that didn't mean she didn't feel it too. "Thank you," she finally said. "For everything."

"No need to thank me," I said. "Really." I rolled my eyes toward the ceiling, glad she couldn't see my face.

"Hey, Brent?"

"Yeah?"

"Can you tell me if anything important happens at the meeting today?"

I nodded. "I'll tell you." Seth's words about her working with Kieran against us rang in my head, but I quickly brushed it off. I trusted Zoe, with all my heart. Besides, Kieran wasn't against us. I would have to get used to that idea again, but I believed it.

"Thank you." She slowly pulled away from me and stood. "I should get going before Seth shows up. I'm glad I have you in my life." She opened the window and disappeared out the window and down the tree.

Little did she know, she'd taken my heart with her. I hated being the good guy. The understanding guy. The one not to cause trouble.

How was I supposed to win her over?

Chapter Nine

Zoe

I managed to get out of Brent's just as I heard Seth's car down the road. I jumped out of the tree and broke into a run, turning the corner before he came within sight. He hopefully had no idea I had come. If he went into Brent's room, he might sense me. Crap! I hadn't thought of that.

I slowed my run to a walk and waited for my heart to slow down. No one was following me. I banged the heel of my hand against my forehead. I was such an idiot! Had I really just kissed him? Twice? On the cheek, but still. Really? He probably thought I was trying to manipulate him.

I hadn't been! I just thought it was incredibly sweet of him to help me even knowing I was in love with Kieran. I stared at the snow on the ground around me. How had I not realized he liked me? I should have known... sensed it. He deserved someone better than me. Someone sweet. I liked him to bits but I couldn't leave Kieran on his own.

I stopped walking. *Kieran knew!* He'd told me before he left Brent would take care of me. He knew and he hadn't tried to stop him. What the heck?! I started walking again, my steps hurried in the snow.

I didn't want Brent to think I was trying to manipulate him. I really found him sweet and if he had asked me out, I probably would have said yes. I had never considered. I should have, he was pretty cute. Heidi liked him, I was sure of it.

My walk turned into a run as I headed home. After months of working out, as well as my enhanced abilities, running fast and for a long time left me only slightly winded, even though my ears rang from the wind. Even with the training and meditation I did, it was still difficult to tune out some noises.

Dad wasn't home when I got there. He had wanted to get back to work as soon as possible and went straight for the doctor's office after the plane landed. Always a workaholic. I smiled. I came inside and stopped suddenly.

Someone was upstairs.

In my room. I could hear a heartbeat and slow, steady breathing.

I could now detect differences in heartbeats and regular patterns between males and females, and it was definitely a man. Not Dad, though. The heartbeat was too slow and strong to be his. Someone younger.

"Kieran," I whispered.

Only those of us with enhanced physical abilities had such slow resting heartbeats.

I headed up the stairs slowly, just in case. I paused outside my room. "You can't keep showing up like this." I stepped in my room. Kieran sat on my bed.

He jumped up and opened his arms. "I missed you, lass."

I wanted to do nothing more than wrap my arms around him and let him comfort me, but I forced myself to step back. "Sit, Kieran." I pointed to the chair by my desk. "I'm not happy with you."

He sat back down on the bed, looking crestfallen. "Zoe? Why don't you believe me?"

"I believe you." I sighed. Brent. Kieran. Kieran, Brent. When had the complicated become more complex? I thought about Brent's argument. "But that doesn't mean I'm not still ticked at you." I sat down in my desk chair and glared at him. "Either you start telling me what the hell happened, or you have no right to talk to me again. You got it?"

"I didn't want to endanger you." Kieran looked exhausted. "You have to believe me."

"You lied to me, Kieran. More than once. I can't trust you anymore."

Kieran stood, as if ready to leave.

I jumped up and pushed him back on the bed. "I'm not finished." Anger and anxiety that had been welling up inside of me exploded. "Which means I'm not inclined to believe much of what you say. Before all of this went south, you should have told me about your father. I don't like being lied to."

"I didn't lie to you, Zoe." He hesitated and then sighed. "Not really. I just shaded the truth a little."

"Is there a difference?" I yelled, then forced myself to calm my heart and lower my voice. I sat back down on the desk chair. "Get the hell out or tell me what's going on."

He sighed and ran his fingers through his hair, his hand shaking as he rested his elbows on his knees. "What do you want to know? I'll tell you everything. Scout's honor." He held up two fingers and quickly let his hand drop.

This was it. The moment of truth.

I swallowed. "Did you kill your father?"

"Yes." He stared at me with the broken soul of a lost boy. He blinked and made his face unreadable. "I didn't lie when I told you he kidnapped me and drove me to the mine in the trunk of his car. He was going to kill me. I knew it. I wasn't going to let him win." His eyes glistened but no tears fell. "He was completely, bloody mad. I kept trying to get away. I didn't want to hurt him, I really didn't, but he kept coming at me and—" He shut his eyes tightly, a shudder running through his body. "I knew something was within my reach when I fell. I knew what was going to happen." He inhaled sharply. "I could sense it all. This thing at the mine that happened to me, it's no gift. It's a nightmare every day, watching things before they happen or sensing what people are going to say." He pushed his shoulders back and straightened. "My dad had the tire iron in his hand, swinging it like a cricket bat. I grabbed a rock and rolled just as he swung at my head. I... I hit him and ran. I threw the rock and hit him square in the head. He fell back and... and..." He punched his knee with his fist. "I panicked." He stood and began pacing. "I can't be deported, Zoe. I can't go to jail. I won't survive. I'm not a juvy, I'd be tried as an adult." He shook his head. "I knew everything, the outcome of the court case, everything before it even happened. So I hid the body and made up the story about him being in Scotland."

I swallowed. "You don't know everything. You couldn't have sensed the court case. You imagined it."

"I guess that's between my brain and my conscience to decide."

I stared at him, his gaze never wavering as he met my eyes. "What about the break-ins? Did you do those? Did you attack Brent's dad?"

"No," he said. "I mean yes. I mean..." He sighed and then started again. "I only broke into a few stores so I still had some money to live off of. But I never broke into any of those houses, and I wouldn't have ever hurt Brent's father. I mean it, Zoe. Only a few stores and that was only temporary, anyway. I tried the lottery. Comes in handy when you can sense winning tickets. All I took was enough to keep me afloat until college."

I really wanted to believe him. He was still everything to me, even though I had no idea if I could ever trust him again. Fate really was a bitch with a sick sense of humor, wasn't she? "What about Rylee?" I whispered. "She figured it out. She knew you had killed your dad. It makes sense that you..."

His look stopped me cold.

"I can't believe you, Zoe," Kieran spat, rage filling his eyes. "Out of everyone, you think I'm monstrous enough to—"

"You admitted it to me that night!"

"No! I told you I felt responsible. I still do. I should have sensed what was going to happen sooner. I could have protected her." He jumped up, anger filling the room enough that I could hear it. "It's my fault. If I hadn't hidden my ability, I could have figured out a way to protect her. We all could have stopped it."

"All of us?" I snapped, guilt taking over reason. "So you built lies upon lies and now Rylee's death was an accident too?"

He stared at me in disgust, or was it disappointment? "No, I didn't bloody kill her! I meant it when I said I would never hurt any of you. I've been trying to figure out who the hell did."

I raised an eyebrow. "You've been carrying out your own investigation?"

"Don't sound so surprised." He crossed his arms over his chest, his muscles a momentary distraction before I refocused. "She was my friend, too. Besides, being a fugitive isn't nearly as exciting as it seems in the movies."

"If she was your friend and you claim you didn't do it, why don't you bring your work over here, then? Maybe I can help you. Maybe all of us can."

Kieran nodded slowly. "That's why I'm telling you this. I want you to help. And I think you can."

"If I'm going to help you, then Brent needs to know also." Seth was not a good person to enlist at the moment, and Heidi would tell him if we excluded him. "Brent can help too."

Kieran's upper lip curled. "Really?" A single eyebrow rose on his chiseled face. "Brent's not going to help me. He wants you to himself."

"I know," I said.

Kieran rolled his eyes. "It was obvious, Zoe. You don't need a sixth sense to figure that one out. He's a swell guy, but his poker face is as strong as the protection under a Scot's kilt."

I flushed. Was I the only one who had no idea that he liked me?

Kieran must have misread my red face. "Have you and him... you know?"

I shook my head. I didn't want to admit it to him, but I couldn't stop myself. "It doesn't matter." I glared at him. "You told me to have Brent take care of me, remember? He can't do that if he doesn't have all the facts." Not to mention that with the suspicion being thrown on me by Seth, it didn't look like I was really betraying them. "Brent deserves your trust. He can help you."

He sighed. "Fine," he said. "I'll go with my gut-feeling."

I raised an eyebrow at him.

"It was a joke." In a flash, Kieran pulled me into his arms. He kissed me lightly on my lips. "I still hope one day I can truly have you again." He sighed and then released me, leaving me longing to be in his arms again and have his lips on mine. "I should go. You can fill Brent in. I'll be in touch."

Someone was pulling into the driveway. I nodded and crossed my arms, as if that would protect me from the waves of emotions rolling through me right now.

He walked out of my bedroom door and I sat down on my bed, far away from where he was sitting. Despite myself, I listened to Kieran as he walked out the back door without stopping. I told myself it was because I wanted to make sure he got out all right without getting caught. Not because I wanted to make sure he didn't steal anything on the way out.

Chapter Ten

Brent
The meeting accomplished nothing important. Seth spent half the time spewing out more gibberish about how we needed to get Kieran and take care of it ourselves. I don't get what had happened to him. He seemed to have changed so much in the past five months.

Seth wanted to check the mine for more clues. He was adamant about it. Now that the cops had cleared the area, everyone could go up there freely again. I doubted Seth would find anything and told him so. He threw me a disgusted look and hopped in his mom's truck, roaring off in the direction of the mine.

After he had left, Heidi and I tried to figure out how we could get Seth to come back to his senses. Aside from telling his father and strongly encouraging getting Seth enrolled in therapy, we couldn't think of anything.

"I doubt he'd be open to seeing a therapist," Heidi said. "I'm getting sick of seeing them myself."

I nodded. My parents didn't make me see a therapist, but I was definitely getting sick of seeing the inside of the office of the grief counselor at school. "Maybe we should get him a therapy dog."

"Really?" Heidi rolled her eyes. "That's your solution? Therapy dogs are cute, but they won't replace Rylee."

"You think we should try and get him a girlfriend?" I stared at Heidi. If she did have a thing for Seth, then she now had no competition. It would be her chance to get closer to him.

Heidi shook her head. "Not fair to Seth or the girl. No one wants to date someone pining for another girl."

I nodded. Good point. "We should ask Zoe what she thinks we should do. He's not listening to us."

"We can't do much right now. Everything's all messed and screwed up. We should be moving forward. It's frustrating." She stood, stretched, and picked up her purse. "I should go. Call me if you want to talk or you see something up with Seth, or... whatever." She shrugged and looked down at the ground as she walked out.

"You too." I couldn't believe she hadn't tried to argue and say Seth was fine. She usually sided with him these days. "And Heidi?"

She turned back to look at me. "Yes?"

"Thank you," I said. "For believing me about Seth. I'm glad I wasn't imagining the whole thing."

She smiled slightly at me. "Thanks for being here to talk to."

As Heidi pulled out and left, my dad pulled in from work. He looked exhausted. "How was your vacation?"

I shook his hand, forcing my face to appear normal as my supernatural ability picked up a notch. "It was good."

"I'm glad to hear it." He yawned. "Do you think you can tell me all about it in the morning? I'm really tired."

"Yeah," I said, trying to figure out why he would want to head to bed at supper time. "Where's mom? I haven't seen her today."

"She's probably in her room." Dad locked his car door as we headed inside. "You know how she gets once a month."

I nodded, totally grossed out. She would have come rushing down to see me if she was home. Something else was going on. Dad wasn't looking me in the eye. Mom would rather go out and get lunch with friends or go to the tennis courts than sit in her room and ruin her figure with a tub of ice cream and reruns of *Cheers* and not greet her son. "Okay," I said. "Well, see you in the morning."

"See you in the morning."

No mention of dinner? We weren't the happy go-lucky family but Mom never missed anything. She was the glue that kept us together. I headed up to my room and picked up my guitar. Mom was supposedly in her room, huh? I could check that easily enough. I set the guitar down and headed down the hall. Mom and Dad's room was on the end of the upstairs. All it would take was a quick run of my fingers on their wall.

My stocking feet were silent on the carpeted hallway floor. I paused outside their door and listened for any sounds coming from the other side. I avoided seeing through my parent's bedroom at all costs when there was a chance both of them were in there for obvious reasons. When I didn't hear anything, I figured it was safe. I lightly touched the wooden door with the tip of my finger. Immediately the solid wood became like painted glass. I could see inside the room but I could also see the door right in front of it. Inside, Dad sat on the foot of the bed, taking off his socks and shoes. He was alone in the room and the picture of him and Mom that usually sat on display on the nightstand was now resting face down.

Where the hell was Mom?

Chapter Eleven

"What's going on, Zoe?" I asked. "You look really nervous." I had been waiting for third period study hall all morning. I wanted to tell her about my folks. My mom never came home last night.

We were back at school. Life had tentatively returned to normal with classes resuming after the winter break.

Zoe and I have the same study hall on Mondays. Judging by the way she was slowly ripping up a notebook page, school was the last thing on her mind. Her hair was thrown up in a lopsided ponytail and she was wearing a wrinkled t-shirt and no makeup. Zoe rarely treated school like a fashion show, but she usually made an effort to be presentable unless something was wrong. Like there clearly was now.

She looked at me and bit her lip before picking up her pen. Our study hall supervisor had a strict no talking rule. Everyone around us was already absorbed in something else and not paying any attention to us. If she was writing it down, then it had to be pretty important.

She slid her notebook over to me. *I saw Kieran yesterday.*

I stared at her message. She still had contact with Kieran. Of course she did. He was in love with her and she was in love with him. If Kieran needed help he would contact Zoe. I looked at her. She looked so nervous, wondering what I would think of her. I wrote back: *He's back in town?*

He's doing an investigation into Rylee's death so he can clear his name and catch the real killer. He wants me to help. I told him I would only help if you also helped.

My brow furrowed. *Why do you want me?*

We need you. I need you. I would rather not feel like I was completely betraying the team by telling no one else. Seth can't know about it. He already thinks I'm out to kill everyone. Besides, I'm not sure I want to be alone with Kieran right now.

I raised an eyebrow at the last comment. Why the hell would she not want to be alone with Kieran? She wasn't afraid of him. She couldn't be. Even I could see Kieran would never hurt her, even if he did kill Rylee. She had to be mad at him. I realized, to my surprise, that I wasn't happy by that fact. Heidi was right. You don't want someone pining after someone else. Even if she was mad at him now, once his name clears they'll resolve their conflicts and be a couple again. There was no use pretending that I had a chance with her. I wrote down my response quickly before I could change my mind. *Sure. When should we meet?*

Zoe shrugged and then started writing. *How about tomorrow afternoon? I don't know how to get in touch with Kieran except wait for him to break into my house again.*

I nodded. "Why not today after school?"

A loud "Shhh!!" from the teacher shut my question down.

"Because my dad asked me to ask you, Seth, and Heidi if all of us could come to his office and get some bloodwork done," she whispered back.

Chapter Twelve

Zoe

After school, Heidi and I took the Beetle and met Seth and Brent at Dad's office. Seth refused to ride with us and Brent had gone off to talk to him. Apparently he couldn't catch up with him because Brent showed up shortly after Seth, obviously in a different vehicle. Seth sat on a chair in the far corner, glaring at me out of the corner of his eye. He didn't just suspect me anymore. He'd made up his mind.

Heidi looked at Seth and then exchanged glances with Brent. Eleanor, Dad's nurse, tried to clear the uncomfortable silence. "Zoe!" she said in an annoyingly cheerful voice reserved for patients. "Your dad's just finishing up with a patient right now. He'll see you and," she glanced down at the chair and continued in a surprised voice, "all your friends, shortly." She looked me up and down before she stood and went back to check on Dad, or do whatever she did when she left her desk. Probably had to clear a patient room and make it big enough to hold the four of us.

"What the hell?" I muttered.

"What?" asked Brent.

"I don't know," I said. "Usually she's annoyed when I'm here. My Dad probably told her she had to be nice to us. I don't think she's ever called me by my first name before."

"Maybe she had her coffee today," Heidi teased.

"Or even something stronger," Seth added.

We all looked up at the same time and over at him. For the first time that day, he smiled. But it was still a bitter smirk without an ounce of happiness in it. Instead of talking and joking around like we used to, we pretended the others didn't exist.

That's what had become of us now. It was as if we weren't even really friends anymore. We were just trying to coexist for the time being while we tried to figure out what else we could do.

Eleanor didn't return to the waiting room and luckily no other patients came in either. Half an hour later, Dad called us in. "How was school today, kids?" he asked. "I hope it wasn't too hard being back."

"No," I said. "It was school, sort of boring."

"Seriously boring," said Seth, yawning. "I fell asleep in like three classes. It's as if the teachers have perfected their monotone over the break."

Dad smiled. "Don't take it for granted. Someday you'll miss it all, even the monotones."

"I doubt it," Seth said. "There isn't much of high school I want to remember."

"You know that's not true," Heidi said, lightly punching his shoulder "You love high school. You keep saying that you never want to graduate and grow up."

He fixed her with a glare. "That was before."

"Well, I'm glad the day wasn't too stressful." Dad avoided the argument and redirected us to a patient room I hadn't noticed before. It was larger, with two tables to lie on and four chairs, plus his desk unit and rolling stool. He pulled a tablet out of his desk drawer. "Brent, could you roll your shirt sleeve up? I'm going to take blood from you first." He set the tablet on the counter and typed in a password. A screen with the five of us showed up, Rylee included. I blinked and turned away.

Eleanor came in, then, to help. She stared at all of us with annoyed interest as Dad took our pulses and blood pressure and several vials of blood. Eleanor arranged the vials of blood very carefully while he did it.

As he took our blood, he shot out a series of questions. "How do you feel? Any fever? Racing heart? Odd dreams? Followed by a hundred other typical doctor questions that we basically all answered no to. He marked everything off on the tablet.

"Okay, guys." Dad pulled his gloves off and tossed them into the appropriate trash. "Thanks. You're all free to go."

I rubbed the smiley face Band-Aid pinching the crook of my arm. "Hey, Dad, can I talk to you for a second?" I waved goodbye to the others as they left and then shut the door in Eleanor's face so Dad and I were alone in the office.

"What's up?" He slid the tablet into his drawer and locked it. "Is everything okay with you and your friends? All of you were really quiet today compared to Mexico."

"I know." I sighed. "It's complicated. A lot of bad memories being stirred up." I waved my hand. "I wanted to ask you something else. A while back you said my blood had merged unusually with the radium in the mine, right? To create some sort of halo around my red blood cells."

"Yes." He nodded at the vials. "I'm checking to see if all of you have the same thing or if they've merged differently on each of you."

"Would it be possible to separate the radium from my blood?"

"You want to get rid of your powers?" Dad's brow furrowed. "Zoe, this is a pretty serious thing you're talking about here. You won't ever be able to get them back. The odds of recreating the exact same conditions with the mine and the lightning storm are next to impossible."

"I know." He didn't get it. He thought it was all scientifically amazing. "But I want them gone. I don't want them anymore. I want to be normal."

He looked ready to argue with me. I could hear it in the way his breathing changed, his heart rate increased and the vessels around his heart constricted. He made a physical effort to control himself. He understood it was my choice in the end, not his. "I'll look into it."

"Thanks, Dad." I hugged him and he held me longer than necessary.

"I love you, sweetie."

"Me, too, Dad."

Out of the office and back in the waiting room, Eleanor sat behind the desk. "Your friends left." That was it. No good-bye. No interest except in the popping of her bubble gum.

"Okay." I grabbed my coat and scarf and left.

Outside, it had started snowing again. When I walked to my car I found someone had cleared all the snow off. "Thanks, Brent." I smiled and reached to unlock the door. It was already open. I must've forgotten to lock it when Heidi and I arrived. I got in and reached to start the car, trying to get the cold air to turn warm.

I nearly jumped when I saw someone sitting in the passenger seat. "Crap!" I punched the visor.

Kieran rubbed his arm. "You know these old cars are easy to break into."

I started the car and sighed. "You can't just keep popping in. Someone's going to notice."

"I'm not planning to make a habit of it." He grinned. "You look pretty with a knitted hat and scarf and red nose." He pressed his lips in a straight line when I didn't return his smile. "I didn't tell you where I'm staying." He handed me a folded piece of paper. "This is the address of the motel where I've set up camp. It's only in the next town over and they let me pay in cash. If you need to reach me, you can call me there. Ask for Jamie Frasier."

"Seriously?" I said. "Jamie Frasier? Watching a little bit too much *Outlander*, are you?"

He smirked. "Don't be ridiculous. I have loads of things to do while holed up in a crap motel and snow falling outside." He shrugged. "I read the books and watch the show. Have you talked to Brent?"

"He agreed to help us."

"Zoe?!" Brent's voice called out in the parking lot, as if on cue, toward the car. I unrolled my window.

Kieran stiffened beside me. "So much for meeting tomorrow."

How'd he know I told Brent to—of course, sixth sense.

Brent squatted down by the window. "I just came by to ch—" He noticed Kieran. "Hey."

"Hi." Kieran stared at him with guarded interest.

"You shouldn't be here." Brent's voice came out as guarded as Kieran looked.

"I was just leaving."

My head moved back and forth like watching a tennis match. "He wanted to know where to meet." It sounded lame.

"Well," Brent said and straightened, "hurry it up. I'll wait in my car for you and make sure you get home safely." He turned and headed away before I could reply.

"He's not too happy with me." Kieran fixed the rear-view mirror so he could watch Brent. "Let's meet tomorrow at the motel." His face softened into a brief smile as he reached to stroke my cheek. "Please get some rest tonight, Zoe. I don't want you up all night worrying."

I bit my lip and nodded. I had the impulse to hug him and tell him everything that was happening in Elliot Lake and how Brent apparently had a crush on me and how Seth was losing it and my Dad knew everything. I stopped myself. Even if I wasn't still mad at him, he couldn't stay here just to gossip. He needed to get going. I reached for his hand, slid my gloved fingers between his.

He squeezed my hand. "I should go," Kieran said as he stared at our hands. "While the coast is still clear."

I nodded. Could he see everything I was feeling? Sense everything that was going on? Like how much seeing him again tied my stomach into knots of longing and hurt.

He leaned toward me and hugged me, his lips brushing lighting against mine. I closed my eyes to kiss him again when suddenly all that I felt was cool air and the sound of the car door closing and crunching footfalls in the snow drifting away. I sat staring at the parked cars in the lot. A whiff of his scent still hung inside the Beetle. I inhaled deeply. It seemed familiar and yet so foreign to me.

I wished, I really wished, there was someone left I could really talk to.

After school the next day, I plugged the address of the motel into my phone GPS. "I'm glad we're taking my car," I said to Brent. "This is definitely a sketchy place."

"Are you sure it's safe for us to go there? I should've come here on my own."

"We'll be fine. We're superheroes, remember?" I joked. "With all of the training we've been doing, we can take care of ourselves in case something comes up."

"I guess." He shook his head. "It still seems dangerous to me."

"Well," I said, putting my seatbelt on, "it is dangerous. We'll have to be alert while we're there. But I think after the fire from the water tower, the attack of the diner, and well, recent events, a sketchy motel of druggies and prostitutes seems to fit in with the new norm."

"Yeah, except we've already lost one of us." Brent sighed. "If we believe Kieran didn't kill Rylee, and he's going to try and convince us. We need to find out who did. Before they start picking off all of us, one by one."

I stared at him in surprise. "We'll be fine," I repeated as I pulled out of the school parking lot and we made our way through the streets and to the highway. "Have you and Heidi talked to Seth's dad?"

"Heidi did, during her study hall today. She called his mom, actually." Brent moved his fingers like he was playing an air guitar with one hand. "Apparently Seth's signed up for therapy, but he hasn't been going. He's been spending more and more time in his room. His mom's going to bug him to go today."

"He's eighteen. No one can force him to go to the meetings."

"No," Brent agreed. "His mom's super cool. He'll listen to her. I know Heidi's going to stop by his place and talk to him today. Maybe go with him if he wants."

"What about you?" I asked. "The two of you used to be pretty close. What's happening to us?"

"Not that close." He sighed. "Everything's changed since the mine."

I couldn't deny that. Everything had changed. For better or worse.

Chapter Thirteen

Seth

"I wanted to try out this new cookie recipe," Heidi babbled, sounding nervous. "You were the first person I thought of for taste-testing since my dad's allergic to chocolate and my mom won't eat sweets."

"Sure." I sat in Heidi's kitchen as she mixed ingredients in a bowl. The scents of dark chocolate, eggs, sugar, and butter assaulted my nose, but it smelled good.

Unfortunately, they weren't the only scents. It didn't cover up Heidi's perfume which had to be pure essential oils from lilacs because I couldn't smell any chemicals mixed with it. Citrus cleaner covered the wooden table, countertops and somewhere down the hall was definitely a dirty laundry basket that needed to be tended to. It had taken a while for my stomach to get used to my new power nose, but at least I didn't get nauseous anymore.

It didn't stop me from wrinkling my nose at the one unpleasant scent I could detect.

Heidi saw my face. "It's the dirty laundry, isn't it?" She set the spoon down. "I've been tasting sweat and dirt from it all for about a week now. Maybe two."

"I'll believe it!" I shook my head. "Why the hell don't the people in your house do laundry? Is your washer broken?"

"No, but it's hard for us to keep up on household tasks." Heidi grew quiet. "Dad's away on business all the time, and my mom's been taking on extra shifts to help me with college tuition. I was the main one who did the chores before, but lately it seems like I can't find the time between my own work and... other stuff."

I felt a small stab of jealousy about her going to college. I wanted to go and got into a few of the ones I applied for. At the very least I'd have to defer for a year to work. I know Dad wanted to help me out, but he really wasn't able to. At least not enough. He and mom worked hard, barely enough to pay the mortgage and put food on the table without trying to come up with an extra twenty grand for me to go. It didn't matter. I wasn't meant to escape the shit-town of Elliot Lake. Unlike Brent, who had ridiculously too much money. "I didn't know you were working. When did you start?"

"Only a few weeks ago. I'm working at Moody's Diner now. Only on the weekends while school is still in session but it's better than nothing."

"That's cool." Poor Heidi stuck in a food joint. Our senses should be making us money, not costing us. "I don't suppose they're hiring other people at the moment, are they?"

"I don't think so." She laughed. "It stinks, you wouldn't want to work there. But the bookstore across the street is."

I wrinkled my nose. Books and I didn't get along. "I'll keep looking."

"I didn't realize you've been looking for a job," Heidi said.

"I have to get one if I ever want to go to college," I said as I watched her check the oven. "But I haven't gotten that serious about applying yet." I had applied to a few places before the mine incident and a couple after that. But after Rylee died... the thought of working and college seemed trivial. I cleared my throat. I knew better than to think of her. Whenever I did I stopped thinking straight. In fact, I just stopped thinking. Period. Problem was, it was impossible not to. I still didn't want to accept the fact she was gone. "What type of cookies did you say these were?" I asked, changing the subject.

"Chocolate chip peanut butter. It looked interesting."

"I like peanut butter cups, so I'm sure I'll like these."

"Great!" Heidi smiled. "Thanks again for being my guinea pig. I'd eat them myself, but..."

"You'd traumatize yourself if they were bad." I smirked. "I understand. That's why I no longer smell milk to see if it's still drinkable."

Heidi chuckled and kept mixing. I watched as she worked, and appreciated the fact that she wasn't trying to talk to me about Rylee or how well I was grieving or any bullshit like that. All my father was preoccupied with was how I was going to move on from Rylee. Hell, even Brent reeked of concern for my well-being. Did they all think I was supposed to move on from Rylee just like that? Why couldn't I grieve for her at my own pace? Why was it so bad that I wanted to see the son of a bitch who killed her face punishment for what he had done?

Heidi was like a breath of fresh air. She smelled mostly of lilacs and discomfort, which was her usual smell. I was pretty sure being around other people made her nervous, especially one on one with them. Since figuring that out I had made a small effort not to be as, well, *myself*, around her, but I could still smell the slightly bitter scent of anxiety.

She put the cookies in the oven and then started to clean up. The smells of baking ingredients became the smell of Dawn dish detergent. I helped her wipe down the table and put the dirty dishes into the dishwasher. The cookies had to cook for at least fifteen minutes. What were we going to do during that time?

Heidi seemed to have a plan. "I don't know about you, but I'm definitely ready for a taste of normalcy. We have Netflix hooked up to the TV. Want to watch something while we wait?"

I hesitated. Normalcy did sound nice. In fact, it sounded fantastic. But I knew it would only be temporary. And if we watched something, then I would end up spending a lot longer here than I planned to, which meant I wouldn't be able to search the mine for clues. "I don't know," I hesitated. "I really do have to take off after the cookies come out."

"Okay." Heidi tried to hide her disappointment but I could sense it. "We'll stop the movie when the cookies are done and we can finish the movie whenever. Or not. I don't care. It beats just sitting here and doing nothing, right?" Her anxiety increased. Probably the thought of fifteen minutes of conversation made her want to pass out.

I reluctantly nodded. "Okay," I said. "What do you want to watch?"

She smiled at me and the sweet smell of relief filled my nostrils. "We'll find something," she said.

Chapter Fourteen

Zoe

Kieran led both of us into the sparse but oddly clean motel room. After years of growing up in his father's filth, I doubted he would ever live even slightly messy again. "Come on," he said by way of greeting. "Before someone sees you."

I looked around the room. On the bed was an open suitcase with files and notebooks strewn about. Near it was a beat-up old laptop open to a page on a freelancing website. "So that's how you make your money now," I said, going over to it.

Kieran nodded. "It's the least conspicuous."

I saw a muscle in Brent's jaw tighten and heard his heart rate increase. He stopped himself from saying whatever it was that he wanted to say.

"How do you keep the cops from finding out?" I asked, quickly directing the conversation away from Brent starting a fight.

"My freelancer name and the name for my profile account are both Jamie Frasier." Kieran shrugged and tried to smile. It didn't reach his eyes. "If anyone bigger than the Elliot Lake police department was looking for me, then it probably wouldn't fly, but I haven't been caught yet."

Brent moved some of the files on the bed to the floor and sat down. "What's all this?" He pointed to the papers. "Are these police files?"

"Yeah." Kieran nodded. "I broke in and made some copies of them. The only person there at night is a deputy who falls asleep around eleven. They don't even use security cameras in the evidence department."

"You seriously stole police property?" I shook my head and sighed. "Kieran, do you want to get caught? That was stupid of you."

"I needed the information." He shrugged. "I needed to know what the police know. Not just to protect myself, but so I can figure out who killed Rylee." He hesitated and glanced quickly at Brent, who again opened his mouth and then shut it tightly, his side muscle twitching again by his jaw. "They got a detailed look at the crime scene, I didn't."

I glared at him. "That was still stupid, not to mention wrong."

"What else was he going to do, Zoe?" Brent picked up one of the files. "If he's not guilty, it's a smart move. Someone needs to solve this case." He flipped through the file in his hand. "What do they say?"

"That she was killed in a hit and run. Forensics determined the car was blue. There are photos." He swallowed hard. "Don't look at them."

Brent quickly shut the file and dropped it like it burned his fingers. I knew why, he could see through the manila folder with his hands.

Kieran cleared his throat. "They found blue paint chips and marked it down that it may be a Toyota Camry. An earlier model, like from the late nineties. There were marks in the snow from the tires that makes them sure it was deliberate. They believe—sorry, they theorize—the car accelerated but it's hard to confirm because of the snow falling that night. Rylee was," Kieran's voice lowered, "hit head on and thrown into the air. The report says the cops are still looking for it but, its whereabouts are unknown. That's all in that file." Kieran pointed to the file at Brent's feet. "According to another file, they are possibly ruling me out as a suspect for her death. I don't own a Camry and they have no reason to believe I had a motive. But I'm not out of the woods. Because I ran and nobody came forward as my alibi, I'm still a possible suspect they would like to call in for questioning. However, it's in my father's case I'm the main suspect."

"That's this file, I'm guessing," I said, picking it up. I opened it and quickly covered the picture with my hand. I didn't need to see a dead body mutilated by a rock and then nature. I quickly scanned the police report. I already knew Kieran was guilty on this one and it seemed like the police knew it as well. However, there was no motive listed, nor was there any information on the physical abuse. Without that information, they would find Kieran guilty for murder for sure. "Kieran—"

"I know," he said. "I'll turn myself in as soon as we find Rylee's killer."

"How are we even going to catch a killer?" Brent asked. "We can't just waltz up to the police station with a person bound and gagged in our trunk and say 'we stole police files and found this person guilty'. That's not how it works."

"That's what this is for." Kieran unzipped a side pocket of a suitcase and pulled out a small tape recorder. "I picked this up at Goodwill. It works, has fresh batteries and a cassette. We can get a confession."

Brent scoffed. "That still doesn't explain how we're going to get it to the police, or help in any way."

"We'll cross that bridge when we come to it," Kieran argued. "First, we need to find out who it is." He pulled a map out from under the bed and spread it out on the comforter, showing Elliot Lake. "This is what I've figured out so far."

It was a shot of the day of Rylee's death, more or less. Tacks pierced the map with different labels, showing us, my father, and Rylee. I saw myself at home, as well as Brent, Seth, and Heidi at their respective homes. Kieran was pegged up at the mine and Rylee's tack was where her body had been found. There was a red arrow pointing up the street. *Direction of vehicle?* written in red ink right beside it.

"Because of the side of the road she was on, it makes more sense the vehicle came up behind her. You were talking to her on the phone, Zoe," he said, looking at me. "You told the police that she showed no sign of seeing a car come at her. If that's correct, then there's no way a car could have been coming in the opposite direction. It would have been driving on the wrong side of the road or it would have left skid marks from suddenly turning that way. Where the car came from and where it went later is still a mystery, but it would have to have been ditched quickly after that because it was banged up."

"What makes you think it was banged up?" I asked.

"Shards from headlights and pieces of paint were found on Rylee's body and on the tree nearby," Brent said, turning a page in the police file he had opened again. "That's how they have a good idea on the make and model of the car. Kieran's right. There's no way the killer would have been able to drive that car for very long afterwards. Not without being noticed."

"My theory is that he dumped it in the nearby woods somewhere." Kieran drew a line with his finger from the scene of Rylee's death, around a corner and down a back road to the woods surrounding Elliot Lake. "The cops haven't put this together. If we find that car, we have a crime scene that not even the police have been able to touch."

"The killer could've gone back to get rid of it after the buzz died down," Brent said. "What's the chance it's still there?"

"Snow. Bad weather. Cold. It's really difficult to hide a car," Kieran said. "They couldn't have gotten it fixed. Elliot Lake has limited resources, but one of the methods they used listed in the report is sending out notices to all auto-repair places in Elliot Lake and the surrounding towns. In the back is a copy of the notice they sent out. It clearly says that if they don't report a blue Toyota Camry coming in for these repairs, then they'll be charged with obstruction of justice. The killer and the car is still at large, so it's pretty safe to say it wasn't repaired and it's probably rusting in the woods somewhere." He hesitated. "My gut tells me it's in the woods."

Brent raised his eyebrows. "I don't suppose you've checked out the woods, have you?"

Kieran shook his head. "I've looked a bit but I don't know the woods that well. I could easily get lost at night and there are too many people around during the day. That why I need help from the two of you."

Brent nodded. "So you think the car will help us find the killer?"

"It's a start," Kieran said. "Can you guys find this area all right?" He pointed on the map to the woods he believed the car was in.

"Yeah." Brent had stood up when Kieran put the map on the bed, he shivered and shoved his hands into his pockets. "We go hiking in these woods all the time. We don't even need a map to get there."

"Good," Kieran said. "The less of a paper trail there is between you and me, the better. I don't want the two of you to get in trouble on my account."

"Aren't we already risking getting in trouble just by being here?" Brent glanced at me, then back at Kieran.

Kieran fixed him with a hard stare. "I told you, I wouldn't have gotten the two of you involved in the first place if I had a choice. I swear."

Too much testosterone. One of these lions was going to roar and try to pick a fight. I stepped between them. "We'll be careful when we look for the car, okay?"

They both finally nodded. I glanced at my watch. "It's time for us to go. I'll let you know if we find something."

"Thank you, Zoe." Kieran held my gaze before slowly turning to Brent. "You too, Brent. I mean it."

Brent nodded at him.

"Keep her safe."

"You know I will."

I shook my head. I was still in the bloody room and could hear them loud and clear. "See you." I turned and opened the motel room door, too embarrassed to hug or kiss him in front of Brent. It felt wrong after Brent had admitted he had feelings for me. Brent followed me out.

We waited until we were back out into the car with the doors closed and engine running before talking.

"We can't do this tonight," I said. "It's nearly dark and it's too late and my mom's going to be ticked if I get home past curfew. She's basically waiting at the door for me when I'm at her place."

Brent nodded. "That's fine. I have things to do as well. Tomorrow?"

"Yeah," I said, pulling out of the motel parking lot. "I wonder how Heidi did with Seth today. Do you think she was able to keep him from going to the mine?"

"I don't know." Brent stared out the window, his mind seemed a million miles away. "I just hope he trusts her a little more than he trusts the rest of us. I'll even take that."

I turned left at a stop sign. "I guess I'd take that, too. Hopefully she can talk him off the ledge." I glanced at Brent, but he wasn't listening any longer. He was looking in the rear-view mirror with a furrowed brow. "What's wrong?"

"That gray car has been following us since the motel."

I looked in the mirror and saw a small gray vehicle a car back. "They probably pulled out at the same time we did. There's only one way out of this crappy little town."

But as we drove, the car didn't leave us. It kept following us down the road back to Elliot Lake.

"Pull over," Brent said suddenly. "Stop the car. Right now!"

I slammed on the brakes, not even pulling to the side of the road. Brent opened the door before I even realized.

The car whizzed by.

I heard Brent's camera click as he took a picture as the car disappeared in the distance.

"Did you get it?"

"Kind of." He dropped back down into the passenger seat staring at the screen of his phone. "The license plate's blurry but I'll be able to recognize it if we see it again."

"Me too." I shivered. If we knew their car, it was pretty easy to figure they'd know mine. "Now what?" I stared ahead at the empty road in front of us. I could still hear the sound of the gray car's engine as it sped away. I'd never catch it in my little Beetle.

"Now, to the school to get my car."

I nodded. "Sounds good."

Chapter Fifteen

Brent

Mom and Dad were both home by the time I pulled my car into the driveway. I could hear them in their room, talking in hushed voices. I sighed in frustration, annoyed they were trying to hide something, Kieran was trying to hide something, and everyone had freakin' secrets. I didn't announce I was home. Instead I walked up quickly and listened, trying to make out what they were saying.

"What're you going to tell them, John? How are you going to tell our boys you want a divorce?" his mom hissed.

I blinked in surprise. I'd never heard my mom ticked, nor did I see divorce a part of the equation. What had his dad done now? I pressed my fingers lightly on the door seeing the scene closed off in front of me. My father stood by the window smoking and my mother sat on the bed, her hands gesturing as she spoke.

"I don't know, Karen. What're you going to tell them? That you've been screwing your tennis instructor for the past five fucking years?"

Mom coiled back like she'd been slapped. Her face burned red as she stood. "Maybe I wouldn't have started the affair if you were ever at home. I'm not your wife, I'm your little trophy! Where've you been, John? Do you even know me anymore? Do you even know your sons?"

Brent swallowed. The words sinking in. My mom's been having an affair? Was that where she was the other night? Unable to listen or watch anymore, I stalked off to my own room, wanting to slam the door, but closing it quietly instead. My family was being ripped apart and there wasn't anything I could do to stop it. Maybe Zoe was right about the powers. What was the point of having them when I couldn't even stop my own life from going to hell?

The next day I sat with Heidi at lunch. "How did it go?"

She knew what I was referring to and glanced around the near-empty hallway where we sat eating just to make sure nobody was listening. She shrugged. "I was able to get him to watch a movie with me. We made cookies, too. It was late by the time he went home so I doubt he went to the mine."

I grinned. "Nice job." I punched her lightly on the shoulder. "Way to go, soldier."

She smiled. "I think he wants things to go back to normal. It's just hard without any closure on Rylee's death." She leaned her head against the locker. "Her superficial crazy nature drove me bonkers at times but I would do anything to hear her voice again."

I nodded. "Me, too." I stared at the half-eaten sandwich in my hand. "Seth too."

"I told him I'd come over to his house today and I was going to bake him something else."

"Save me some?"

She gave me a small smile. "Have you seen the size of Seth? Good luck on that."

After school, Zoe and I took her car down the road Rylee was killed on. Neither of us could bear to look at the tree stump that was all that was left to mark her grave. For a while there was a small memorial for her with candles and flowers, but it was taken away or buried in snow while we had been in Mexico. Even with the memorial gone, it was still too painful for either of us to look at it. So we just looked at the road ahead and turned down a side road that led to the forest.

We parked the car at the edge of the woods and got out.

"We'll cover more ground if we split up," Zoe said.

"I'm not letting you go on your own. Someone could be here."

She looked at me with the odd way she had. "And you don't think I'll hear them long before they hear me?"

"True."

"And you don't think I can outrun or scream out to you?"

I sighed. She wasn't going to budge on this one. "Does your cell have service?"

"Yeah," she said, smiling smugly. "It does. Yours?"

"Uh-huh."

"If we find the car or get lost, then we call each other. If not, meet back here in an hour, no matter what?"

"Sounds good," I said, sighing. I had hoped we could walk together so I could tell her about my parents. Hers were divorced. Maybe she could shed some light on the stupid subject. I turned and headed to the right of where the car was parked. Maybe not mentioning it would stop it from happening.

I kept my eyes trained to the ground to see if I could find anything like tire tracks, even though I knew I wouldn't. It had been over a month since Rylee was killed and since then it had snowed, rained and snowed again. There would definitely be no clear tracks. However, a car was heavy and would crush tall grass, vegetation and even possibly scrape some trees when driven off the path. I was sure they'd have ditched it the night of the accident, probably even shut off the lights.

I glanced up at the mine off in the distance. You could make out the outline of it through the barren trees. Something caught my eye and I moved quickly to have a closer look.

A piece of bark had been scraped off the side of a tree, about headlight height of a car.

I kept going, hurrying forward and growing frustrated when I couldn't find anything.

I threw my hands in the air, looking around the woods before checking the time on my watch. I had been looking for over half an hour and I still hadn't found anything else besides the stupid bark mark.

My phone suddenly vibrated.

I flipped it on, turning to run back toward the car. "Zoe? Everything okay? You lost? Someone following you? Did you hurt yourself?"

"Not at all!" Zoe laughed. She sounded giddy. "I found the car!"

"Really? Where?" I sped my pace and veered toward the direction she had started searching in.

"I can hear you running. You're not far from me. Keep coming straight in the direction you're going, it'll be on your left."

Before long a dark blue blob came into view. Definitely a beat-up old car. As I ran closer, I could tell it was a Toyota Camry. It had a huge dent in its hood and a broken headlight. The license plates had been ripped off.

Excitement and revulsion filled me. I stuttered to a stop, gasping for air but not really winded. We could actually get somewhere in the investigation, but I couldn't help but picture Rylee being crushed by this car. "I can't believe it," I finally said. "Kieran was right."

Zoe stood a few yards to the left of me, her hands shoved deep into her pockets. "Come on." She walked up and peered through the car's window before checking the door.

"You think touching it is smart?" We'd be leaving fingerprints.

"I don't care. We found it, we're going to check for clues." She stared at me. "You want to call the police first?"

I shook my head. I pulled my phone out to take pictures. The car's hood, the car from a distance, and then the car's interior. Aside from being slightly mildewed at being exposed to the elements for so long, there really wasn't anything exciting or telling about the inside of the car. Whoever had done this had thought ahead. Not so much as a disposable coffee cup lay in the car. Even the glove box was empty. Not even the car's instruction manual or the registration sat in the glove box. Nothing.

The thing was beat up and old on the outside, printless and perfectly clean on the inside. Well, not clean, but clueless.

"This is insane!" I groaned in frustration. "It's definitely the car, but there's nothing here. I bet the person has even wiped off the prints, not that we'd know what to do with those anyway."

"The person would have had to dispose of the contents of the car somehow." Zoe looked around. "Even if the car's clean, there's a registration." She checked the driver's door and front window before swearing under her breath. "Gone! Damn car id's gone, the licence plates, everything!"

"Fire?" I suggested.

Zoe's head shot up and then she slowly nodded. "You think?"

"That's what I would have done."

"The killer probably disposed of them as soon as possible," she said.

"This whole area outside of the forest part is a campground." I gestured around us. "It shouldn't be hard to find a fire pit. Do you think the killer would've been sloppy enough to leave some of the evidence unburnt?"

Zoe shrugged and began walking to where the treeline thinned. "We might as well check it out."

Neither one of us looked back as we left the car.

The last thing we wanted was to see its damaged hood again.

The closest fire pit was a short walk from the dumped car. I knelt down in front of the fire pit. It was full of damp ash and partially burned wood. I picked up a fistful of it with my hand

and ran it through my fingers. When I did, a piece of metal cut my skin. "Shit!" I sucked my cut finger to stop the flow of blood.

Zoe carefully used a stick to clear the ash. Blackened thin metal showed in the pit. "It's part of a license plate."

We both began sifting through the ash, throwing any piece of metal we found to the side. After we had gone through it all, we stared at the half-formed licence plate. It was futile. The characters were illegible. I took pictures of it anyway.

"There's nothing here." Zoe shivered and looked up at the gray skies and sun just peeking through. "Let's go. We can come back tomorrow."

"Wait, hold on!" Something caught the weak sunlight, like a quick sparkle. I jumped into the pit and picked it up. It was the top part of the key. "The rest must have burned or broke away. Probably the ash piled up and kept this piece from melting." Unlike the license plate, this piece of key looked nearly undamaged by the fire. As I turned it in my palm, I saw flecks of something on it. "It's painted pink," I said, peering with my eyes and trying to see if I could make sense of it with my super-vision. "That's not part of the key, is it?"

"No." Zoe leaned in to see it as well. "I've a feeling that the killer labels their keys by painting them different colors." She smiled at her silly analogy. "It's something, at least," she said. "More than the police have."

I took pictures of both sides of the key and then put it in my pocket. "You think it's enough to catch the guy?"

"It's a start," Zoe said. "Let's get out of here before—" She hesitated before I heard what she was listening for.

A twig snapped. We both turned to see someone disappearing through the trees. "Get to the car, Zoe. Now!" I yelled, running in the direction the person was going.

Zoe passed me as I ran, mumbling something about not letting me catch the dickhead alone.

We sprinted to where the person was disappearing through the woods. We gained ground on him fast. With our enhanced abilities and our training, there were very few people who could outrun us.

Except something was wrong. Whoever this person was, they were a lot more used to the woods than we were. While we were constantly tripping over roots and running into trees, the person in front of us had no trouble at all. We caught up just as they dove into a car and sped away, leaving us behind.

Panting, we stared at the small gray car as it sped down the road.

"We're definitely being followed." I looked at Zoe and reached for her hand.

Whoever it was, knew we were on to them.

Chapter Sixteen

Zoe

The day after we found the key, Brent called everyone in for a training session. The first in a very long time. Since Rylee's death, we'd been training on our own, but our hearts weren't in it so we didn't organize anything. We were tired of playing superhero and angry with each other. I didn't think we could spend two hours in Brent's gym without a fight breaking out. I continued working at honing my hearing so I could tune things out or focus on one thing better and I'm sure the others were doing the same thing at least a little so we could survive in the human world all right. Brent let me use the hyperbaric chamber and it helped. It just reminded me of Kieran so I had been avoiding it.

Brent sent everyone a text to meet out where we had parked the Beetle yesterday, just outside the forest by the mine.

"Why'd you call us here?" Heidi rubbed her arms. "It's cold out and everything tastes like dirt." She shivered slightly and looked around the forest.

"Here," Seth said, taking off his jacket. "I'm getting overheated anyway." He handed it to her. "Besides, I needed a reason to show off these babies." He flexed his muscles under his tight, long-sleeved black shirt and kissed his biceps.

Heidi and Brent laughed, but I rolled my eyes. I knew he was making an effort to be civil today, at least to Heidi, but I was still angry at him for thinking I would betray them all. Not to mention his witch hunt for Kieran. We'd just have to prove him wrong.

"I thought it would be good for us to get back in sync with each other," Brent said. "We need to keep training. A run in the woods would be a good way for us to figure some things out."

I knew a run in the woods to bond over wasn't all he wanted. I didn't know why he had called us out here at all for a training session, but I could tell that for some reason he needed it, as if he just didn't want to go home. We had the key, would he mention it? Would he purposely run them by the abandoned car? I bit back saying something, not wanting to draw any more attention to myself, or possibly Kieran.

Seth, through his fog of self-absorption, must have noticed it too. "I'm up for it," Seth said. "It's nice to be challenged now and then. Besides, everything here smells nice. Except for you, of course." He pointed to Brent and snickered. Brent punched him in the arm.

I watched their interaction. Seth seemed his old self in a way. At least with Heidi and now Brent as well.

"Let's get going." Brent broke into a jog.

The rest of us quickly followed suit. The frigid air cut through the school warm-ups Brent had taken from storage near the gymnasium. Because all of the athletic teams got new warm-ups every year, four sets of five-year-old warm-up suits weren't going to go missing. It was better than any workout clothes we had for jogging through winter weather.

We all struggled to keep pace with Brent. We tripped over different roots and dips in the ground, buried under the thin layer of snow. Cold moisture seeped through our sneakers, but aside from that the run was almost pleasant. Brent pushed the pace, stumbling but never stopping. I liked listening to the sound of the forest around us, as well as all four of our heartbeats and labored breathing. There was even something peaceful about it.

I continually checked around and behind to see if anyone was following us. No additional heart rate added to the four of ours, nor did I hear anything out of the ordinary. I stayed alert nonetheless.

Twenty minutes into the run, Seth and Heidi fell behind a ways. I moved up beside Brent and let the gap grow.

Brent noticed it too. "Do you think we should wait?"

I focused on Seth and Heidi and listened to them talking behind us.

"You're quiet today," Heidi was saying. "And you're in a good mood. What's up? Wake up on the right side of the bed today?"

I smiled and Brent gave me a look. "She's teasing him," I informed, blushing slightly to be caught eavesdropping.

Seth laughed. "I'm glad we're training. I'd have chosen something other than a nice run in the woods. But it's still invigorating."

"It's cold, wet. I'd rather be in the gym. What's with Brent today?" Heidi asked Seth.

"Dunno," Seth said. "But I missed all of this. I wish we had never stopped in the first place. I guess it just didn't seem right, after... well, you know."

I shook my head, focussing back on Brent's heartbeat. "Let's give them their space." I didn't want to listen to them. It wasn't my business. Talking about Kieran was my business, this was not. "Seth's opening up to Heidi."

"Yeah." Brent hopped over a large root. "Well, Heidi's nice. She's a good listener."

A stab of jealousy shot through me. Was it possible he liked her? I mean, what wasn't to like? He was right. She was nice, and a good listener. She was very quiet and laid-back, not to mention beautiful. There wasn't any reason why he wouldn't like her. I bit the inside of my cheek. I had no right to be jealous... and yet I was. The thought of it made my stomach turn. I still loved Kieran, but was it possible I had feelings for Brent as well? *Life is so damn confusing.* Rylee would have loved it. She craved drama like some people craved chocolate. It was ironic that the most drama happening to us happened after she died. She was probably watching us from the afterlife, laughing.

"What're you thinking about?" Brent chuckled. "You're smiling."

"I am?" I tried to relax my face. "Nothing. Just... nothing. Hey, where're we going?"

"I figured we could run up to the parking lot of the mine and circle back," Brent said. "We would have been running for a few miles at that point, which is a pretty decent workout."

"That's true," I said. "No car?"

"You mean the gray one?"

"No, the abandoned one."

"Not today. I don't think trying to explain how we know all the police reports and about the car is going to work without getting Seth riled up."

"I agree."

"You haven't seen the gray car again, have you?"

I shook my head. "I've been keeping an eye out for it, but so far there's been no sign of it anywhere." I listened around us again. "Nothing here today either."

Brent nodded. "Hopefully they were scared away by us nearly catching them. I still think you should let me drive you. They saw both of us, but it's your car they followed." He'd tried arguing with me last night on the phone, but I had refused.

"For all we know, they're following your car, too," I argued again. "Or they're watching my house. It doesn't matter, I doubt switching cars would fool whoever is following us. It might just make things worse."

"We have these superpowers, who it is doesn't have anything."

"Maybe it's a newspaper reporter trying to get a story."

He shrugged, clearly not buying it. "If Kieran didn't kill Rylee, someone did. I don't believe for a minute it was an accident because of the weather. I agree with Kieran on this. Someone knows."

"How could they?"

"Your dad knows."

"That's because he took my blood. I'm his daughter! He tested me. He's a doctor!"

Brent raised his hands. "I don't think it's your dad!"

"I know that! I'm just..." I rolled my eyes. "I'm just defending him."

"I know." He smiled. "So, I'll pick you up tomorrow then?"

"I can't just be dependent on you for rides," I said. "It's nice of you, but I would feel bad."

"It's not about feeling good or bad." He moved closer to me. "I want to make sure you're safe."

"I am." I stumbled over a dip in the ground and Brent caught me from falling. "If I see the car around again, I'll park the Beetle in the garage. Okay?"

"Promise?" Brent asked, raising an eyebrow.

I jerked suddenly when he pushed me. "Wha—!" A large tree split between us. Had he not pushed me, I'd have run straight into it. I laughed suddenly when we joined back together. "We definitely need more training time in the woods. This has to be one of the toughest workouts I've ever done."

"No kidding!" Brent nodded. "And dangerous. That tree almost took you out!"

I glanced at him from the corner of my eye and saw him laughing. "What's with your idea behind training outside in the cold?" I heard Heidi moan again about her feet starting to freeze.

"I like training." Brent refused to look at me. "I wanted to today. We can't actually set up the gym again for a while, but just training feels like old times, you know? It feels normal. All I wanted was a sense of normalcy."

I nodded, but I was concerned all the same. Brent hadn't sounded this troubled in a long time. "What's wrong?"

He clenched his jaw and shook his head. "I'll tell you later. I-I don't want to talk about it right now. Let's just enjoy the run."

Something was definitely wrong but I knew better than to push him. Instead, we kept running. We stopped in the mine parking lot and waited for Seth and Heidi to catch up.

Seth put his hands on his knees, breathing hard. "That was fantastic!" He straightened and beat his chest. "We're superheroes again!" He tried to pump his fist in the air with a devilish grin, but the effect was ruined by the fact he was still out of breath.

Heidi panted beside him. "You sure picked a hell of a workout, Brent."

Brent grinned. "We should do it again."

"Not now!" Heidi looked mortified.

I was about to agree when I heard something that made me stand straight up. "Hey guys," I whispered. "I hear something."

"Not surprising," Seth joked. "You're always hearing something. A squirrel probably sneezed."

I heard it again, this time louder. "Help!" someone was shouting.

"What is it?" asked Heidi.

"Someone needs our help." I circled, trying to locate the cry. "Badly."

"Which direction?" Brent bent down and touched the ground.

I closed my eyes again, focusing on the plea. "That way." I pointed to the right, off into the woods.

We all tore off running in the woods as fast as possible. I couldn't hear the person cry out again and I feared the worst. The last cry had been faint, even for me, and we were all out of breath after our run. I hoped we got there in time. I prayed I was leading everyone in the correct direction.

Seth shouted, "I smell something!" He veered slightly to the left and we all followed him through the woods. "It's a woman!" He leapt over a tree stump. "I think she's being attacked."

As we got closer I heard the sounds of struggling and a woman crying out, followed by a scream. "Come on!" I sprinted as hard as I could.

Brent and Seth were the fastest, neck and neck for the lead.

"I see her!" Brent called out.

The woman was a distance away, running in the opposite direction. Away from us.

"We're here to help!" Seth called out to her. "Are you all right?"

Suddenly the ground gave way below us. Screams pierced my ears as we fell and I covered my ears with my hands, but my head felt like it was going to explode from the pure noise, all up close. Then pain exploded in my head and everything went black.

Chapter Seventeen

Kieran

The feeling came suddenly, sending my body into a cold chill. The vision appeared suddenly, warning me of Zoe's imminent danger. I tore myself away from my laptop, knocking it to the ground with half of the papers on the bed. I didn't bother to pick them up as I grabbed my shoes and raced out the door.

Zoe was in trouble. All I cared about was getting to her.

They were in the woods, I knew that for sure. All of them had run right into a trap. Where in the woods, I wasn't sure, though. Nor could I see who set the trap. "Bloody hell," I muttered as I strapped on my motorcycle helmet. I was going to need help on this one. Who in Elliot Lake could I even go to for help?

I didn't have to think twice. I turned down the road to Zoe's dad's office. As far as his daughter was concerned, nothing was more important. Hopefully that meant he would listen to me and help me without asking questions about whether or not I was a crazy lunatic.

I sped through the streets and parked the bike in a doctor's marked parking spot near the front before I raced through the front of the building toward her dad's office.

His nurse-secretary lady wasn't there, so I headed straight toward the back, to his office. Shouting, "Doc? Hey! Zoe's dad?" I opened the door without knocking.

He looked up, shocked. A pair of Beats earphones covered his ears. He must've been dictating or something. "Kieran," he said, pulling the earphones off. "What the h—? What're you doing here?"

"Zoe's in trouble," I said, nearly smiling that he caught himself from swearing. "Don't ask me how I know because I can't explain it. But she's definitely in trouble. Big trouble."

He paled and then grabbed his keys. "Where is she?"

"By the mine."

He raced out of the office, quickly locking the door. I led the way down the stairs and into the parking lot.

"We'll take my car," he said when he noticed my bike.

I followed him, focussing on trying to sense anything else about Zoe. I couldn't and it was driving me nuts. "Oye!"

"Pardon?" Zoe's dad unlocked his car and we jumped into it. He tore out of the parking lot and headed toward the mine.

"Nothing, sorry. Just frustrated." Part of me wondered why he believed me and why he wasn't taking me directly to the police.

"You have the same ability as the others?"

I stared at him as houses whipped by. "Um... no?" When had Zoe told him? Or had he known all along.

He glanced at me from the corner of his eye. "Your bloodwork showed nothing. Did it occur later?"

I shook my head. "I switched my blood that day."

"Really?"

"Just a hunch I needed to." I shrugged and we drove in silence the rest of the way.

Zoe's dad drove to the edge of the woods to where Brent's car and the Beetle were. As soon as the BMW was in park, we jumped out.

"Shite!" I swore. "I don't know these woods very well. I know she's in the woods, but that's it. Damn it!"

"Calm down." Zoe's dad put his hand on my shoulder. "Push your ability and search again."

"It's complicated." I jerked away from him. "No offense, but you wouldn't understand."

"I'm the only one who knows. They're all sense related. What's your power?"

I didn't have a choice. I'd pulled him out to the mine and he'd followed without question. He either thought I planned to kill him, if he believed I'd hurt Rylee, or he believed the bloodwork. The science. "Psychic," I told him. "I can see the future. But my power is a lot weaker than theirs. I only see bits and pieces. I can't control it at all. I saw Zoe, Brent, Seth, and Heidi walk into a trap and now they're in danger! I know they were in the woods. I think they were wearing some sort of athletic gear or something."

"Zoe told me they were going on a run in the forest," he said. "They don't have athletic suits, though."

"They were bright red," I said. "The school's maybe?"

"Must be. At least we can find them easily."

Both of us started hurrying toward the woods.

"They would have turned back at the mine," Zoe's dad said. "Let's start there. We might be able to find something."

Even though we made decent time, I had no idea if it was good enough. I hadn't had another vision. They could be fine or they could be slowly being slaughtered. I couldn't have anything happen to Zoe. I would die without her. Just where the hell were they? "Zoe?" I shouted.

Her father called out and looked around, hoping someone would respond as much as I did.

When we reached the mine parking lot, I noticed several sets of footprints. "This way!" I pointed at them. "Thank bloody goodness for fresh snow!" I broke out into a run.

"Hold up!" Zoe's dad cried, lagging behind me. "I'm not as young and fit as you are."

"There's no time," I called back over my shoulder. "Who knows what's happening to them! You'll catch up."

He nodded, gasping for breath.

I broke into a hard sprint, leaving him further behind. I looked around for any sign of red clothing, but I couldn't see anything. Then the ground took a sharp dip and I slipped, sliding down, and landing in a pile of leaves.

I stood and looked up to the sky, too far up to crawl out. I dusted the leaves off me and swore under my breath, "Bloody hell!" Zoe's dad was going to have to go searching for them till I figured a way out.

"Kieran?" a voice whispered faintly.

I swung around. "Zoe?" I followed her weak voice and dropped down beside her. "What happened?"

"You found me."

"Of course." I tucked a strand of hair behind her ear and pulled a dried leaf out of it. "That's quite the red suit." I glanced down and then ran my eyes over her stomach again, almost missing the blood because of the darkness and the red. I didn't even notice the others in the pit. All I noticed was her. "What the hell happened?" I lifted her shirt and saw the gash. I stood, looking for something to press against the wound.

"You're what happened, you son of a bitch!" Seth tackled me from the side, knocking me to the ground. Sharp pain hit my elbow but I ignored it and got to my feet, swinging a punch at him. I didn't have the training like the others did, and Seth had size and athletics on his side. He easily avoided me and pulled me into a headlock. "Why'd you come back?" he hissed. "Why the hell did you trap us? Wasn't it bad enough you took Rylee?" He kicked me in the groin and I groaned before doubling over.

"Seth, stop it!" Zoe cried. "He didn't kill Rylee!"

"Shut up, Zoe," Seth spat. "I know he did." He kicked me in the ribs as hard as he could. "He's a damn monster who's going to pay for what he's done, one way or another."

"I didn't kill her!" I groaned, gasping for breath. "I'd never do that."

But he ignored me and kicked me harder.

"Seth," Heidi said, grabbing his arm. "Stop it."

Seth hesitated and looked at her before looking at me and growing more enraged. "He trapped you in here, too," he said, pulling his leg back to kick me again.

Suddenly, Brent came out of nowhere and tackled Seth to the ground, punching him in the face. "Lay off, man," Brent hissed. "You're not helping anyone right now. We're stuck here, he is too!"

Seth held his nose.

"You're only upsetting Heidi, not Kicran."

Seth looked at Heidi, saw she was crying and went still. I realized that I was more out of the loop than I thought with my friends. My gut told me they were falling for each other, just hadn't admitted it to themselves or each other yet.

Zoe hobbled over to me. "How did you find us?"

I sat up, my head spinning and my side aching. "I sensed it," I mumbled. "You okay?" I reached for her, trying to check her side but the spinning had me reaching for air. "What happened?"

Seth mumbled, "You know." Brent kicked him in the side to warn him to shut up.

Zoe shook her head. "I don't know." She grimaced as she shifted to reach for my hand. "One minute we were jogging. Then we heard someone cry for help. We rushed over and the next moment we fell in here." She looked around at the clearly man-made walls and the tarp covered in brush and snow that had fooled them into thinking it was solid ground. Part of it must have originally been a mine tunnel. The top cover having been done recently. A classic trap. "I guess maybe that person wasn't in as much distress as we thought."

"Zoe-zey?" Her dad's head appeared at the top of the hole. "Are you kids okay?" he called down.

"We are," Zoe called out. "Slightly bruised but everyone's okay."

"I'll run back to the car and grab the cables and rope."

I laughed. "You have rope in your trunk?"

"I'm a doctor." Zoe's dad squinted into the dark. "I have everything. Seth? You down there?"

"I tham." The sound came out very nasal.

"Should I call your dad?"

"I'm othay," Seth mumbled and had to repeat it so Zoe's dad could hear.

"Did you break your septum?"

"Huh?"

"It sounds like your nose is broken."

"Oh yeah." Seth glanced at Brent. "It happened when I fell."

No one spoke as we waited for the rope to climb out. I tried to ask what happened but Seth refused to let anyone talk. I didn't argue. I had to prove myself to him and Heidi.

After Zoe's dad helped all of us out of the hole, he took one look at our injuries and declared that all of us were going to his office immediately. "When we're there, you can tell me what the hell's going on." He pressed a towel on Zoe's glaring red cut and tossed the other to Seth.

"It's not our fault, Dad!" Zoe tried to explain.

"All I know is that Kieran isn't as innocent as his blood results made him out to be."

I blushed slightly at that statement. I guess Zoe hadn't told him that I switched the test results. That wasn't going to be a fun conversation. Right now he didn't want to kill me. I didn't know how he would be after I told him. *If* I told him. He might hate me as much as Seth did.

"Let's go." Her dad tied the rope and walked slowly as we made our way back to the car. "Zoe, you're driving with me. Brent and Kieran can go in your car. Seth, I need to set your nose. It's going to hurt like hell but I have to do it before we drive back."

Brent and I reached for the driver's door at the same time.

"Right." I nodded and strode around the car to the passenger's side. Zoe tossed him the keys but I didn't miss the long look she gave me, even though I pretended not to notice. Her dad was ticked, I wasn't about to piss him off any more.

I heard Seth grunt and cry out when Zoe's dad set his nose as we pulled out of the parking area.

We drove the first bit in silence. No music, not talking. Brent kept tapping his thumb against the steering wheel and I was near ready to break it.

"We were here yesterday. Zoe and I."

"You were?" I swung around to look at him. Why hadn't either of them told me?

"We found the car."

"You're shittin' me." I had a super sixth sense and it didn't let me know that? The one thing I've been focussing on the past two months?

Brent shook his head, keeping his eyes on the road. "Zoe took pictures but it's been abandoned. And cleaned. Someone made sure there was no evidence left inside of it. We did find a burnt license plate that might be related." He swallowed, his jawline tight. "And a key."

"What the hell?" I punched my knee. "Where's the key?"

"At my place."

"Let's go get it." Why hadn't they told me this? "Why the hell did you think it was a good idea to go running by the mine, the day after you went digging for evidence? How stupid are you? It doesn't take common sense... unless you were planning on having Seth and Heidi find the car by mistake?"

Brent's jaw muscle twitched right on the spot he'd been tightening a moment earlier. "I just wanted to run. We weren't looking for the car."

I dropped back against the seat, folding my arms over my chest. "We need to know what that key's for. Is it a car key?"

"I've got pictures of it on my phone."

Did the guy not know the difference between a house key and a car key? I shook my head. "Let's go check it out."

Brent sighed. "After. We need to head to Dr. Landers' office first. I'm not raising any flags or causing any problems there."

Don't want to ruin your chances with Zoe? I bit my tongue and held the words back. The freakin' guy had no clue. Absolutely no clue.

Neither of us spoke the rest of the drive to the doctor's office.

Zoe's dad waited until all of us were in his personal office before he shut the door. "What in Sam's name is going on with you kids?" He turned to me. "And when did you get back into town? Or did you never leave?"

"We heard someone calling for help," Brent said, laying down on one of the two checkup tables. "Or Zoe did, really." He closed his eyes and rubbed his forehead. "Hey, I'm feeling a little dizzy. Is that normal?"

"You might have a concussion. You shouldn't have driven." Dr. Landers came over to check Brent. "Does anything hurt?"

"I've a headache and my arm does," Brent said.

"Take off your jacket. You probably got banged up in the fall." He lifted Brent's arm and turned it to look closer at the inside of his elbow. "Zoe, take your jacket off."

"Uh, okay." Zoe pulled it off and winced as she did so. I reached over to help her.

Dr. Landers checked her arm and shook his head. "Heidi, Seth, let me see yours."

I watched them all, trying to figure out what was going on. So was everyone else.

Each of them had identical wounds in the crooks of their right arms.

"What the hell have you guys gotten mixed up in," he whispered, grabbing antiseptic wipes and bandages.

"What's going on?" I asked. "What is it?"

"These aren't cuts from the fall," Dr. Landers said, wiping his daughter's arm first. "These are pinpricks made by syringes. Someone's been taking your blood."

I ripped my long sleeve off and stood shirtless in the room. I heard Zoe's breath suck in as I checked my arm. Nothing.

"What?" Zoe asked, her voice an octave higher than usual. "What type of sick and twisted person would do that?"

"Have any of you told anyone about your powers?" Dr. Landers asked. "Is there anyone any of you can think of that might possibly know about them at all. If so, you need to talk now."

All of us shook our heads, Seth took a moment to throw a glare my way.

"No one," Zoe confirmed. "As far as I know of. Do you think someone found out?"

"Why else would they go through the effort of trapping you?" Dr. Landers said. "Do any of you remember being knocked out? Or remember someone taking blood?" He looked like he was grasping at straws. "Did any of you feel it? Drawing blood isn't just a simple pin prick."

Rylee. Whoever killed her wanted her blood for her powers. "Could our powers be transferrable by blood?" I asked.

Dr. Landers shook his head. "I've no idea." He gestured to the ground. "In the lab below us, I'm trying to isolate the uranium strand, but it's next to impossible. It's like a halo."

"A radium halo?" The term seemed so familiar to me now.

"I'll have to run some tests to see, but I have no idea how I'll go about it." He sighed. "I'll find out." He finished bandaging up Zoe's cut on her side and checked the small bump on her forehead. "Get some water, honey," he murmured before turning to Brent. "You need to stay hydrated and rest for a while too."

"I'll go grab us some water from the kitchen you've got at the back." She headed out of the room, looking dazed.

I considered following her but Dr. Landers called for me to sit on the table beside Brent. "You look pretty beat up. You're next." I glanced at Seth but said nothing as I sat down on the gurney table.

Brent winced when the antiseptic cloth touched his skin. "Whoever set this up, is Rylee's killer. I'm sure of it."

"That should be easy," Seth mocked. "Since he's sitting in this room right now."

"For the last time I didn't kill her." I flipped him off, tired of defending myself, yet more annoyed that he wasn't going to be the only one who thought I was guilty.

"She found out about your father." Seth crossed his muscular arms over his chest. He wasn't finished with me yet. "She was going to tell all of us and you decided you needed to shut her up."

"She found out by the radio," I retorted, laying down and grimacing at the soreness by my ribs. "The entire county knows it was my father's body at the mine. I was a suspect no matter what. If you think I'm such a self-serving bastard, then why wouldn't I go after you guys straight away?"

"I never said you were smart," Seth said.

"Seth!" Brent hissed. "Would you just listen to yourself for once? And use your friggin' brain. Kieran didn't kill Rylee. It makes no sense why he would. Not even the police think he did."

"How would you know what the police thought?" Seth retorted. "You been hanging with them or peering through walls without us?"

Brent looked away. "I just know."

"Brent?" Dr. Landers turned his chair, scooting over to me but keeping his eyes on Brent. "What aren't you telling us?"

"I stole a couple of police files." I had no intention of letting anyone take the fall for me. "Not stole, really. Copied."

"You did *what*?" everyone, but Brent said at once.

"I told you he was a bad guy." Seth groaned. "And stupid, too. Stupider than me."

"And a murderer!" I snapped back at him. The guy was an idiot. I inhaled a deep breath and caught it as pain shot through my chest. It wasn't broken, but badly bruised, a glimpse of the X-Ray Dr. Landers was going to make me do popped into my head. I sighed. "Look, I'm trying to find Rylee's killer. For her and to clear my name. I needed to know what they knew."

"Just about Rylee?" Seth wasn't going to back down. Maybe he wasn't an idiot like I tagged him for.

"About my father's case and Rylee's case. I've been trying to piece some things together and I think I've found something." I told them everything, including Brent's and Zoe's involvement in it.

"Seriously?" Heidi said. "Brent, why didn't you tell us?"

"Some of us weren't ready to look outside the box." Brent glanced at Seth and continued, anger growing in his words, "We might as well get to the bottom of the whole thing and be done with it. Especially before someone does something stupid and ends up in jail."

"Be done with it?" Seth hissed, stepping toward Brent still sitting on the other table. "Is this like some fucking school project to you, Brent? Rylee was our friend. Now she's dead! Murdered! Be done with it? We're never going to be fucking done with it!" His face burned with indignation and a vein began beating near the top of his forehead. I moved to the other end of the table, not ready for another beating. Visions of my father drunken and angry popped into my head. I was never going to be a victim again. Never.

"Enough, Seth!" Dr. Landers stood and moved to a cabinet with a combination on it. "Compose yourself or I'll poke you with a sedative. No one's dying on my watch."

Silence followed as Seth slowly calmed down. His face returned to its normal color as he glared at me.

"I also suggest you keep your voice down," Dr. Landers said nonchalantly as he moved to tend to me. "We don't know who might be listening."

"Who else is here?" Seth glanced around.

"No one in my office. I don't work Saturdays," Dr. Landers said. "I was thinking more of the neighbors. Go check on Zoe. Make sure she's all right and is resting like she's supposed to in the waiting room."

"I'll go." Brent left, leaving just me, Seth, Doc, and Heidi.

"You're going to need X-Rays." He touched my side. "I'm not sure if you cracked a rib."

"It's fine," I told him. "I've been through worse." I blanked the past out and left my face emotionless. It was easier to do then dealing with doctors. "You should check Heidi and Seth first. Make sure they're all right."

"I'd rather stay here while you treat Seth. Check him first," Heidi said as Dr. Landers turned to point to the other gurney table.

Seth glared at her. "You think I'm off the rails too, don't you?"

"I'm concerned for you." Heidi reached out and then dropped her hand. "There's a difference."

"You think I'm loony."

"I think you're upset, and I hate seeing one of my friends upset."

"You don't have to see it. You can leave."

"And you can stop being a jerk and calm down," Heidi snapped.

Dr. Landers had Seth on the table and bandaged him before swiftly treating Heidi. He sent the two of them out of the room to wait with Zoe and Brent.

He turned to me, still sitting on the white crinkly paper with my shirt off. "I can already tell by the way that you're holding your ribs that Seth did some damage there." He ran his fingers over them, checking carefully before nodding. "I've got an X-Ray machine in the other room. I'm assuming you said they aren't cracked because we already checked?" He was referring to my sense ability.

I nodded.

"Then I recommend Advil and not getting beat up any time soon." He grinned. "I'm sure you'll understand if I ask you to get it elsewhere. I know my daughter wouldn't be helping you unless you were planning on turning yourself in after you find Rylee's killer, and I'd appreciate it if I wasn't charged with aiding a fugitive."

"Understood," I said, sliding off the table. "When did you figure out Zoe was helping me?"

"Mexico. If you needed help, my daughter would be the first one you looked to for it. Besides, how else did Brent know what was in the police files when you were the one who stole them?" He looked at me sternly as I put my shirt back on. "I really hope you are planning on turning yourself in, Kieran. If you don't, then I'll go to the police myself."

I nodded. "I will. But I need to find Rylee's killer, first." I hadn't thought about after, only about finding Rylee's killer. However, if I ever stood a chance with Zoe, I was going to have to fix what I'd already broken.

"I think you should let the police do their work. They know what they're doing."

"They don't!" I argued. "They haven't found the car yet." I didn't mention what Brent had told me in the Beetle. No sense in getting Zoe's dad involved any more than he already was. "Besides, they don't know about the powers, nor would they believe us if we told them. There's a whole 'nother level involved that the police don't know anything about. They think they're looking for a driver too cowardly to face their responsibility, but I believe Rylee was killed for her powers. I'm surer of it now than ever after today."

He looked uncertain. "You kids should not be mixed up in this. It can only end badly."

"I need to find justice." I headed toward the door, no intention of getting the X-Rays now. "I can't turn myself in knowing someone is out there, hunting us. I can't..." I swallowed hard. "I can't let Zoe die. I will never let that happen." My voice came out as a whisper. I hoped he would understand. He had to.

If Zoe's life wasn't in danger, I would've stopped running a long time ago. At least that's what I told myself.

Dr. Landers looked at me, studying me for a long time. Finally, he nodded. "Okay," he said. "Find the killer and turn them in. Then turn yourself in."

"I intend to." I reached for the door knob. "Am I free to leave?"

Dr. Landers nodded. "I still want the others to stay here for a bit, but you should get out of here. I don't want anyone to get in trouble before they're supposed to."

"I appreciate it." I opened the door and hesitated. "Also, thanks, Dr. Landers."

"For what?"

"For not asking me if I killed my father or not." I smiled at him and then walked out.

In the waiting room, everyone was either sitting down or laying down, still recovering. I glanced at them as I walked to the door. There really wasn't much to say. Anything they wanted to know they could ask Brent and Zoe.

"Kieran, wait," Zoe called out. She came towards me. "We found the car," she said. "And where the killer burned the things inside." She handed me a plastic bag that had part of a key in it as well as a flash drive. "This has all of the pictures on it that we took."

I didn't tell her I already knew. But hadn't Brent said he had the key? Was he trying to protect her from me as well? "Take care, okay?"

She bit her lip. "You too."

I walked out, wondering if I would ever see Zoe again, knowing it would be best for her if I didn't – at least for right now. I'd protect her the rest of my life, even if it meant living in the shadows.

No one was going to hurt her. No one.

Chapter Eighteen

Brent

I got home late, exhausted and hungry. Mom stood in the kitchen, glass of wine in hand waiting for me. "Where have you been?" Her head moved up and then down. "What are you wearing?"

I glanced down at the school warm-up suits. *Shit*. She would know I stole it because I wasn't even in sports. Hell, I had never taken an interest in anything physical at all until Seth had suggested we become superheroes and train. "I went out for a run with some friends." I shrugged. "And this is a school warm-up suit. We didn't have anything better to wear, so we borrowed them."

"You stole them, you mean."

"We're giving them back after we wash them." I moved to the fridge to make a sandwich.

She shook her head. "You can't just go around borrowing other people's property without permission. It's not honest and your father and I raised you better than that."

"It's not honest?" I swung around. "You really want to talk to me about *honesty*? Where's the honesty in you screwing someone other than dad?"

She flinched. "That is none of your business!"

"No shit! Neither one of you bothered to tell me that all of this happened when I was on vacation. I've been home for four days! And I find out because I heard the two of you fighting the other night. So much for honesty in this household." I slammed the fridge shut, my appetite suddenly gone. There were way too many secrets.

"We're not getting a divorce, Brent," Mom said quietly. "Your father and I discussed it and decided that a divorce would be unwise at this time."

"Really?" I said, unable to help myself from feeling relieved. "Great. I'm glad you guys worked it out."

She had the decency to look a little ashamed. "Don't mistake us staying married for anything more than a business deal, Brent," she said. "A divorce would not look good in the eyes of his company, and I don't want to go out and get a job to support myself."

"Oh," I said, feeling deflated and angry again. "Of course. Because that's honest."

Before she could respond, I pushed passed her and hurried upstairs to my room and shut the door before locking it and putting on headphones. The last thing I wanted to do was talk to either of my parents right now. However, I did want to talk to someone. I picked up my phone and send a text to Zoe.

Five minutes later there was a tap on my window.

I opened it and Zoe slipped through. "Hey." She hugged me. "Parents fightin', 'eh?"

I swallowed. "You could say that." I explained what I knew.

"I'm so sorry, Brent." Zoe rubbed my arm. "This must be so hard. I can't even imagine."

"Why not?" I asked. "Your parents divorced, didn't they?"

"Yeah," she said. "That's exactly it. They divorced. They didn't stay in a cold marriage where they make each other and everyone else miserable. That sucks."

"Thanks for coming over. It's nice having someone normal to talk to."

"Yeah," she said, smiling wryly. "I can hear you from a block away, my father is calling us Radium Halos because we're full of electrocuted lightning uranium and the last person I dated is now on the run for murder. I wouldn't exactly call myself normal."

I couldn't help myself. "Dated? As in past tense?"

She sighed and then nodded once. "I decided after today. He needs to get his life sorted. I won't leave him on his own, but I mean, he needs to turn himself in. He should do it now but he's determined to find Rylee's killer. I'm still upset he lied to me and then left the way he did. It just isn't going to work out, right now. Luckily he understands that."

"You deserve better, you know."

She shrugged. "I guess..."

"You do," I confirmed. "Zoe, you're beautiful, smart, funny, everything." She sucked in her breath and I realized I was leaning closer, almost to kiss her. I leaned back quickly. "Sorry, I didn't mean—"

Her lips cut me off. Heat rushed through my body at her touch and I responded instantly, wrapping my arms around her waist and pulling her closer. My fingers traced up her back, through her hair as she pressed closer, kissing me desperately, as if she was trying to escape from real life as much as I wanted to. Finally, I broke off. "Whoa," I gasped. "That was..."

"Incredible," she finished and grinned. "Sorry, I didn't mean to attack you so hard. Everything's just... complicated."

"I don't mind in the slightest," I said. I held her in my arms, enjoying the feeling of her against me. "Are you sure this is what you want?" I hoped she understood the full meaning of my words. I never took kisses casually, especially from her. She could break my heart with a single word.

"I think this is what I want."

I hesitated, my brain racing in one direction, my body in another. "I think we should wait." *What the hell are you doing, dummy?*

"Pardon?"

"I think we should get things sorted. Figure out Rylee, concentrate on school, decide on what university we're going to go to..." *Make sure you're over Kieran.*

"School? University?" Zoe stepped back, her eyebrows high on her forehead. "I don't..." She held her hand up. "Whatever." She moved quickly and swung her leg over the window ledge. "Just forget this happened. Please."

"Zoe! Wait!" What the hell had I just done?

She disappeared down the tree and into the darkness before I could stop her.

Chapter Nineteen

Zoe

What was I thinking? I mean yeah, things were more or less on hold with me and Kieran— probably over for good—but it wasn't even official. Now I'd gone and tried to make out with Brent, knowing how he felt for me? And he shot me down? I jogged faster.

But I couldn't help it. He was being sweet and sexy and sounded so lost and vulnerable. As he was telling me about his parents, all I could think about was what it would feel like to kiss him. So I did. What an idiot! I swore our abilities were beginning to fry out brains.

I felt bad for him, too, though. I had hoped that one day my parents would finally realize that they belonged together and decide to try it again. But having them apart and heartbroken seemed more bearable than staying together and not even trying to work out differences.

Thank goodness it wasn't late. I slowed down a couple houses before Dad's and caught my breath before going inside.

Dad had homemade chicken pot pies ready on the table, my favorite. "Hey, Zoe-zey! Back so soon? How's Brent?"

"Okay." I felt the burn on my face. "Having some trouble at home but aside from that, he's fine." I sat down and drank some water already set out on the table. The pit injury from earlier didn't even seem like it had happened. Dad and I had tried to figure out how they had called for help and came up empty handed. Tomorrow he was going to talk to Seth's dad to go and check the hole out. See if they could find something. We had no clues or evidence to help us at all. No further ahead than this morning and also no idea why someone had taken blood without us knowing. It didn't make sense. None of it.

Neither did me kissing Brent and then being shot down.

Dad raised an eyebrow. "There's something you're not telling me."

"What? I'm not going to tell you what Brent talked to me about." I took a bite of pot pie and chewed. "That's breaking his confidence. It has nothing to do with the team, though. Just normal teenage issues."

"Oh you guys are a team, now, huh?" He raised an eyebrow.

"And you, too. You're an honorary member of it." I winked.

"Yeah, well, we'll discuss your very broad definition of a team later. There's something that happened when you were over there that you can't stop thinking about. I can tell."

I blushed. He could tell? There was no way I was discussing my kissing activities with my dad. "It was nothing," I mumbled.

"Zoe-zey, I can tell when you're lying."

"It's nothing, really." I rolled my eyes. He wasn't going to let it go. "It's just, we both, sort of, well, kissed. Then he shot me down. Basically told me I needed to get over Kieran."

Dad breathed a sigh of relief. "Thank goodness! I thought it was a lot worse for a second."

My face was hot enough to evaporate water, now. "So things are over with Kieran?"

"I guess."

He paused, mid-bite. "What do you mean; you guess?"

"Well, I can't exactly date a fugitive who's about to turn himself in for murder, now can I?"

"I'm not saying I'm really happy with Kieran—believe me, I'm not—but he just risked getting caught to save you, and when I told him to stop chasing Rylee's killer, he told me he couldn't have you in danger. Zoe, he's doing all of this mainly for you. Any chance of him getting off easy if he's found guilty for his father's death is completely gone because he wants to protect you. I think he's worth at least 'It's over, Kieran', before you start making out with other guys."

I pushed away my food, suddenly unable to eat. "You're right. Why do you always have to be right?"

"I'm a doctor, it's my job." He winked at me. "Do you know where Kieran is staying right now?"

I nodded. "Unless he's changed motels."

"I think you should talk to him in the morning. Break it off with him the right way."

Had Dad known this was going to happen? "I will." I sighed, almost ready to cry. Everything sucked. Everything. "I don't think I want to date anyone right now."

"I think that's the best idea you've had tonight."

Figures my dad would say that.

The next morning, I drove up to Kieran's motel alone. As I approached the motel, a police car raced by, its sirens blaring into my sensitive ears. I pulled to the side of the road, trying to calm the ringing inside them and also trying to hear what was going on. Kieran's hotel!

I shoved the car into gear and took off, quickly pulling into the parking lot across the street. The motel was swarming with police cars. People were gathering around, gawking at the raid as residents were marched out of the motel in cuffs.

"What's going on?" I asked a nearby woman.

"Someone tipped off the police about a prostitute ring and a drug organization being run there," she said. "Apparently they found evidence." She shook her head. "Serves them right."

If the police looked into Kieran's room and found the police files on his bed, they'd arrest him.

I watched as a line of prostitutes and junkies were led out struggling and yelling profanities at the cops, some walking out in sullen silence. There was a pause as what seemed to be the last of the criminals were led out. Unable to relax I tried to listen to all the conversations going on around me. The police, the people inside the hotel rooms, the owner of the motel. I could hear officers shouting but could not hear Kieran. Maybe he snuck out before they showed up.

Five officers came out, surrounding someone walking calmly to the car. The familiar heartbeat told me what I didn't want to know. "No!!!!" I whispered, horrified.

Kieran turned and looked right at me as the police led him to a cop car. His expression turned pleading, but I knew it wasn't for his freedom. He was silently telling me to get away from there and solve the murder. Then one of the cops pushed him gently into the car and shut the door and I didn't see him again.

Breathing hard, I did my best to block out my panic and the chaos around me as I turned to my car. He was right. I did need to solve this murder.

I had come to break his heart and he was risking everything to save me. It should be me in the back seat of that cop car. Not him.

When I turned to see the street across from the motel, everything went silent. Or at least it felt like it. Parked across the street was a gray car. I wasn't sure how, but somehow I knew that the driver was behind the anonymous tip to the police. They were watching me right now, knowing I was slowly piecing things together.

The gray car suddenly pulled out onto the street. I ran to the Beetle and quickly got in. I pulled into traffic right behind the gray car and watched as it sped up, pressing on the gas to try and keep up with them. I didn't know what exactly I was going to do with a car chase, but there was no way in hell the driver was going to get away with this. Not now, not ever.

The car swerved and took a wide corner. I couldn't get a view of the license plate or the driver, who was wearing a stupid cap. I followed it on a twisting, curving back road. All of the windows were tinted on the car, even the windshields, despite the law on that. Even so, I could barely make out the figure in the driver's seat. All I could see was they weren't that tall because the back of their head was only a little bit taller than the back of the seat.

I kept following it down the roads. The car took a sharp turn I couldn't make and I kept going forward. I braked and back up, but when I looked down that street, the car was gone. "Damn it!" I shouted.

I covered my face with my hands, trying to calm down. I played the scene over and over again in my mind, trying to pick up sounds or anything I could remember that we could use. No heartbeat or engine or anything sounded familiar to me. I had nothing. Kieran was in jail, the police reports were gone, the key we'd found by the abandoned vehicle was gone. Everything!

I slowly drove back to the main road to head back to Elliot Lake. How were we going to catch Rylee's killer before they caught us?

Chapter Twenty

Heidi

Zoe's text message came through while I was browsing through the jewelry in a shop across the street from Pool Hall Parlour.

Kieran arrested?

My first thought was that Seth had found him and ratted him out. I dismissed the possibility. He was mad, but he wouldn't do that.

I texted her back, asking her what happened next, and then tried to process everything that had happened in the last couple of days. It was still hard for me to picture Kieran back on our side after being angry at him for so long. Even though I wasn't surprised he hadn't killed Rylee, he still lied about having a power, as well as a lot of other things. Now, he was the closest and most capable of us to finding Rylee's killer, and he was gone. I couldn't even imagine what Zoe was feeling.

I picked up a designer necklace, admiring the design of it with a smile. It would be a long time before I could ever afford anything but junk jewelry from a thrift store, but I still liked shiny things. My phone vibrated and I put the necklace back to answer it. "Hello?"

"Heidi," Seth said. "I want to apologize for yesterday. I was unnecessarily rude to you."

I raised an eyebrow. I had no idea why he was apologizing. He avoided it as much as possible. "What did you do?"

"What do you mean? Isn't that what people do? Apologize."

"Seth, no offense, but you're an asshole. To everyone. But me. Why?"

"Well, sorry, I'll make a point to insult your hair next time I see you," he grumbled.

"No, that's not what I meant." I sighed. "Did you have anything to do with Kieran getting arrested?"

"What? No!" A loud breath pushed through the phone. "I can't say I'm not happy, or I wish I called the tip myself, but I didn't."

Well, at least he didn't want to kill him right now. Or he wasn't saying it. "Glad it wasn't you."

"Are you at work right now? I didn't mean to interrupt anything."

"Again with you being nice." I shook my head. "It's freaking me out. Stop it." It actually was. I wasn't sure if he had a personality shift or if he was hiding something from me. Hell, maybe he just really hated me and was polite to me because of that. I picked up a pair of earrings made of semi-precious stones. "You know—"

"Everybody down on the ground!" someone near the counter of the jewelry shop shouted. "This is a robbery!"

I dropped the earrings, terror filling me as I dropped down on my knees, the phone pressed tight against my ear.

"Heidi?" Seth's voice came out panicked. "What's going on? Where are you right now?"

"Jewelry shop across from PHP's. Call the police!" I hung the phone up and set it to vibrate. I peered over the glass counter I was hiding behind and strained to get a look at the robber. It was a middle-aged man with a handgun. He looked ticked and ready to use it. He also had a bag and duct tape. "Everyone hand over your cell phones right now! Toss them over to me unless you want to get shot. While you're at it, give me your wallets, your jewelry, your watches. That's a pretty nice purse you have, miss. Toss that over here too." He kicked a designer handbag belonging to a sniveling woman on the floor. There were only three people in the store shopping.

The store manager stood behind the counter with his hands up. While the robber was turned he reached to press the silent alarm but the man turned and pointed the gun at him. "Get out of there right now! If you make any sudden movements, you're the first to go down, buddy." He looked around the shop. "Everyone against that wall over there." He gestured to the wall by me.

I couldn't move though, crouching behind a display case. I was frozen, my heart pounding and my own breath deafening to my ears. He was going to kill me!

The gunman didn't react. He hadn't even noticed me. He was too focused on taking the cash out of the cash register and throwing it in the sack before moving to the display cases.

It was the only chance I had. The moment of surprise. I hesitated, trying to gather my wits. I'm insane. What the hell am I thinking? I haven't done any real training in over a month.

When all of them were training, I had done some martial arts training and fake fights with the others. But I hadn't been in a fake fight since before Rylee's death and the last time I had really hit someone was when the group of college boys tried to rape a waitress at PHP. That was back when we had first gotten our powers.

The fear in the room left a bitter taste in my mouth, mixed with sweat from the store manager, and from the robber. I could see it glistening off his forehead and for some reason thought it was strange that he wasn't wearing a mask. In the movies that meant he planned to kill all of them. Or maybe he was just stupid. Who robbed a jewelry store in broad daylight, and video cameras?

The man was moving through the display cases, quickly grabbing jewelry and dumping it into his bag, not caring if it tangled or broke. That didn't seem normal. If it got damaged, he would get less money from it. That should matter to him... unless any money was good.

I assumed his shaking hands came from adrenaline, but now I wasn't so sure. Quietly, I opened my mouth and breathed in before almost gagging. In addition to sweat and fear, there was something else on the robber. It was practically smothering me with its cloying taste. I had never smelled it before but I had a pretty good idea what it was.

I tried to remember what Health Class had taught about people going through drug withdrawals. Aside from their judgement going out the window and their desperation to do anything for drugs, I wasn't sure what they were capable of. Bad withdrawals made the body physically ill and weak, which could give me the upper hand when it came down to a fight, but that desperation could make that man do things most humans wouldn't ever do.

I would have to take my chances. He was quickly approaching the display case I was hiding behind and he would notice me for sure then.

Before I could stop myself, I somersaulted out from behind the display case and rushed the man, grabbing the gun out of his hand before he could react, and kneed him in the groin. The man groaned and doubled over. I pulled the bag out of his hand and tossed it aside before grabbing the back of his head and tossing him to the ground.

Not moving. I'd knocked him out in one blow! Adrenalin rushed through my veins as the other customers and owner stayed pressed against the wall. Why weren't they helping?

I went to grab the duct tape he'd left by the cash box when someone suddenly grabbed my ankles.

I lost my balance and fell. I couldn't get my hands in front of me fast enough as my head hit the corner of a case. Pain exploded in my head as warm liquid ran down my cheek.

The robber crawled on top of me, pressing another gun against my temple. "You think you're a hero, bitch," he spat. "Well, you might be tough, but..." His eyes widened when he saw the blood. He reached up with a dirty, shaking hand to touch my face.

It took everything inside of me to stay conscious. Blackness crept in my eyes and I blinked, trying to focus on the robber. I cringed from his touch.

He held the blood up to his bloodshot eyes, inspecting it. He smirked. "So it is real," he whispered, excitement lighting in his eyes. "The radium halos." He licked his finger. "Unbelievable." He patted my head with strange tenderness. "You're going to make me rich, sweetheart."

The salty and drug-filled smell of his sweat, the copper smell of blood, everything landed on my palate and I swallowed, trying not to breathe or taste. Bile rose at the back of my throat and the room began to spin. Had he just licked my blood?

The glass door shattered and the robber suddenly flew off me. I knew it was Seth even as my eyes closed. He kicked the man and knocked him across the room. I tried to roll over and help but now the room spun with my eyes closed. I threw up, all over the floor.

The druggie fired his gun and the shot went wild. People screamed. I forced my eyes open and a blurry image of Seth punched the man in the face over and over until the man's hand went limp and the gun fell to the floor.

Seth stopped and disappeared from view. Suddenly he was gathering me into his arms. "Are you okay?" He touched the bloody smear on my forehead. "I'm going to kill him before the cops even get here."

"No, don't!" I begged, so glad he had come. Slowly the room stopped spinning. I stared at the unconscious man, barely registering the sirens wailing in the distance. "Why did you come? I told you to call the police."

"Well, you know me. I like to play hero." He grinned and pulled a strand of hair from my face. "Besides, no one's going to hurt any of my friends ever again. If I can stop it, I will."

I nodded and then winced from the pain. I tried to smile. "So why do you pretend you're not a good guy?"

"I'm always a good guy," he said. "It's just everyone else who's an asshole."

I smiled and then frowned. "That guy wasn't just here for the jewelry."

"What?"

"He knows about us." *The radium halos. You're going to make me rich, sweetheart.* I clung to Seth and rested my head against his shoulder. "I'm scared."

Chapter Twenty-One

Seth's dad and my parents came to the police station to pick us up after the questioning. My mother almost smothered me with her hug. "I'm so glad you're all right, sweetie. That's so scary."

I nodded shakily. "I'm just glad it's over."

"That was very brave of you. Both of you." My mom finally released her overwhelming-hold on me.

"It was stupid," my father said as he pulled me into a hug, crushing me even more than my mother did. "Don't you ever do anything like that again! I don't want the next call to be from the coroner."

"Goes for you too, Seth," his dad said, still dressed in half of his fireman gear. "That was incredibly stupid. I don't disapprove, but I don't approve of it either." The clap on Seth's back had me thinking he was more proud, than worried.

Seth bear-hugged his father. "It won't happen again."

"With all of the misfortune you guys have been having lately, the last thing either of you need is more trouble," my mother said. "Let's go home. You need to rest. Especially with that bump on your head."

I fingered the bandage near my temple. "I'm fine, Mom. Really." Radium halo blood was already working and healing the bruised bump. I could feel it.

Seth reached for my hand and squeezed it. "I'll talk to you later, okay?"

I nodded. "Thanks again for saving my butt."

"Anytime." He winked at me.

Seth's dad put his arm around his son. "Let's go," he said. "We can—" Just then his pager went off. He swore when he looked at it. "There's a fire across town. I'm still on active duty. Took the company SUV with me here."

"Go, Dad. I'm fine."

"Seth can come over to my house," I said instantly. I looked at him, suddenly unsure. "Unless you want to be alone right now. Then we could take you home."

"You should definitely come over," my mom said. "I can make chicken wings and pizza for dinner."

"You had me at chicken wings." Seth laughed and my mother hugged him.

His dad patted him on the back again. "Thanks!" He practically ran out the door to go do his job.

Mom slipped her sunglasses on. "Let's get you guys home. If this craziness keeps happening in this small little town, I'm going to either have to take anti-anxiety pills, or start drinking vodka."

Seth and I sat in the back of the car while my parents chatted to us from the front. While I appreciated the sense of normalcy, especially after the terror and chaos of earlier, I was still scared and I couldn't shake the feeling that there was something bigger at play than any of us knew about. "I have to talk to you," I whispered to Seth. "Later."

He looked at me, his brow furrowed in concern. "Okay," he mouthed. "Everything all right?"

I shook my head. "I honestly have no idea."

At home, Seth and I took off for the family room, calling out that we were going to watch a movie. I knew they wouldn't bug us.

I switched the TV on and told Seth in hushed tones what the robber had said about my blood.

"Seriously?" Seth said when I'd finished. "He really said radium halos?"

"Yeah. Then he licked his finger and said I was going to make him rich."

"What the hell is that supposed to mean?" He balled his hands into fists. "The guy was a crazy druggie. It means nothing."

"No." I shook my head, still able to sense everything from that moment. "It definitely means something. Don't pull any of that crap on me. You know as well as I do someone *is* after us. Not just Rylee."

He looked at me, fear evident in his eyes. "It could still be nothing."

"But it's not. Someone knows about us and it definitely isn't Kieran."

Seth shrugged. "Maybe there's some kind of black market for our blood. I don't know how, but people know about it and know how to harness it or something."

I shook my head. "How could they have found out?"

"Kieran told them."

I punched Seth in the arm. "You know that's bullshit. Stop blaming the foreigner. You know as well as I do that he didn't set this up."

"I don't know. Neither do you. He says he's back to find out who killed Rylee and clear his name. Today just shows me he's hired idiot thugs to do the job. Maybe he's jealous we all got talents and he didn't."

"He's got a super sense as well. A sixth sense."

Seth stared at me. "I heard Dr. Landers mention it and Kieran saying something, but nobody's got a sixth sense. That's impossible."

"So are super senses."

"Not according to comic books."

"Oh my goodness!" I threw my hands in the air. I had a photographic memory and yet Seth knew everything about comic books.

"Okay. You believe what you want to believe and I'll go with my gut. We'll see who's right in the end."

"We need to text Brent and Zoe about this."

"Be careful," he warned. "Maybe someone's reading our phones. We should call them."

"And someone's after our blood. This isn't a silly game anymore. We're all in danger."

Seth snorted.

"What?"

"Seems Kieran's in the safest spot of all of us. No one can touch him while he's in jail."

"Seth, give it a rest!"

"I'm still mad at him. He betrayed us all. And he killed his dad. Who does that? And I..." He clenched his jaw. "I'm the reason why he was one of us." He dropped his head. "If he hadn't been hanging out with me then he wouldn't have been in the mine that day, and my friends wouldn't have been exposed to him and in danger. He would've been another kid in our school who got into some trouble. Nothing else."

I reached out and squeezed his hand. "It's not your fault, Seth. None of it is your fault."

"He killed his own father. I'm not putting anything past him."

I stayed silent. I was happy Seth had opened up and talked to me this much and I didn't want to push him any more than that. I had a feeling that Kieran's relationship with his father wasn't nearly as close as Seth's was with his father. Even if he did kill his father, Kieran might have had a good reason for it.

"Kids! Dinner's ready!" My mother opened the door to the family room and called down.

I stood. "Let's all meet at Brent's right after school, tomorrow."

"Good idea. But we have to warn them tonight. Who the hell knows who's next on the list." His stomach growled. "Food first. I'm starving and your mom's food smells so good I can taste it."

I giggled and lightly punched his shoulder. "That's your super sense, silly."

"Yeah, and I'm keeping it. Nobody's gonna take it away from me."

Chapter Twenty-Two

Kieran

I didn't care that the holding cell they put me in was cramped, sparse, and filthy. All I cared about was Zoe's safety. I only hoped they could find the killer before the killer took her, or the others, out. I didn't even want Seth dead, although I was pretty sure a good ass-kicking might do him good in the long run.

"Hey, Scott," one of the deputies said. "You've got a roommate for the time being. Don't get too comfortable with him. He'll be gone before you even drag yourself out of bed in the morning." He shoved a greasy man into the cell. The man staggered over to the toilet bowl and threw up in it. I wrinkled my nose and turned away.

The man groaned and collapsed on the floor. "Damn teenage punk," he muttered. Whether he was talking to me or the voices in his head, I had no idea. I did know he was going through withdrawals, though. I saw the same signs I learned to recognize in my father. I had a feeling this man was withdrawing from things a lot stronger than alcohol, though.

He squinted at me with bloodshot eyes. "What the hell are you looking at?"

I sighed and turned to face the wall.

"Hey!" he shouted. "I'm talking to you." I heard him stagger to his feet and come closer to me. "What's a pretty boy like you doing in here anyway?"

I didn't say anything.

"You know why I'm in here?"

"Drugs?" I guessed, turning to face his stinking breath.

He snorted. "You're funny, but stupid. I don't have any drugs. Not on me, and not in my system. That's the problem, though."

That's definitely a *problem*. "So what're you in here for?"

"I robbed a store. Then I got caught. Finally slipped up."

"So you're the one committing all of the robberies around Elliot Lake," I asked, trying to appear like I didn't really care.

He grinned. "Have to support myself somehow. You know how it is."

I almost said I didn't know how it was, and that I wasn't at all like him. But I was. I had broken into some stores myself. Just for food, not drugs. I had committed even more crimes than that to protect others as well as myself. "Yeah, I know how it is."

"You're all right, you know?" He grinned, an ugly gap between two of his teeth. "For a pretty boy, that is." He lay down on the ground beside the bunk cot as if it were a bed. "I'm going to tell you the greatest secret of all time." He burped and then rolled over to the toilet and threw up. The air was filled with a putrid stench and I was more grateful than ever that I didn't have Seth's or Heidi's ability. From the hideous sounds coming from him, I was glad I didn't have Zoe's either. I really hoped the greatest secret of all time produced a bottle of Febreeze and some noise-cancelling headphones out of thin air.

The druggie collapsed against the floor, groaning. "The greatest secret of all time," he said again and laughed. "It'll make me rich. Hell, it'll make you rich if you get lucky enough. Listen up, kid."

"Okay," I said, yawning. "What's the greatest secret?" I prepared myself for the punchline of whatever joke he was setting up.

"Radium halos."

Everything stopped, even my heart. "What did you just say?"

"Ra-di-um ha-los," he repeated slowly. "I don't know the scientific crap about it, but it gives you superpowers. Turns the blood sorta purple, too. A person pumped full of radium halos is worth enough to buy a private island near Hawaii. Hell, you could buy Hawaii." He laughed. "I met one, today. Eleanor said they were real, but I didn't believe her." He held up a grubby hand. "Liquid gold ran down my hand from her head. When I get outta here, I'm gonna find her and then retire." He closed his eyes and curled around the rank toilet in the fetal position. "Liquid purple... crazy shit."

Zoe. He attacked Zoe and made her bleed. How come I hadn't had a premonition about it? I always did when she was in danger. Always. Did she know about the price on her head? She needed to know. She needed to protect herself. They all needed to protect themselves.

I ran to the cell bars. "Officer!" I shouted. "I would like my phone call. NOW!"

Chapter Twenty-Three

Zoe

"Hey, are you all right?" I hugged Heidi briefly and then looked at the bandage on her head that was almost completely hidden by her hair.

"Yeah, I'm fine," she said and gave a small smile. "Um, we're going to have to meet after school today at Brent's. There's something really important Seth and I need to tell you."

I nodded. "Dad almost didn't let me leave the house after Kieran called him. I think he's more freaked out than I am. We might have one more piece to the puzzle of Rylee's death." All I needed now was to find out where exactly it belonged. I grabbed Heidi's arm and pulled her to the edge of the school parking lot. "Just to warn you, the robbery was all over the six o'clock news and on the front page of the newspaper this morning. You and Seth are featured in the story."

She groaned. "Why?"

"You know why." When Heidi didn't show like she understood, I pushed it. I was actually kind of mad they'd made such a big scene out of it. One thing we had focused on was getting in and out quick and unnoticed. "One, you beat the guy up. Two, he apparently got close and personal with you. Sucking your blood according to an eyewitness. Three, Seth then came crashing in to beat him up and save you. The two of you were apparently cuddling and whispering to each other until the cops came. They are calling you Romeo and Juliet."

She groaned again. "This can't be happening. School's supposed to be my place of normalcy."

"Well, normal is apparently warped now."

"Hey," Seth said, joining us. He looked at Heidi's face and his own face clouded over. "What's wrong?"

I tried to hide a smile but failed miserably. "Nothing, Romeo. Nothing." I laughed and walked passed them to go into the school. Heidi would be able to break the news to him.

I knew that the story about Seth and Heidi was entertaining me much more than it should be, but Heidi was right about school being the place of normalcy. Even though the circumstances were far from normal, high school rumors about who was dating was totally normal. It was also a good distraction from the more scary things happening right now. Not the least of which being the price on everyone's heads and Heidi being identified as having radium halos. When Kieran had called Dad, I couldn't believe it. Dad sat down and told me about it and he admitted that there was a possibility of there being a strong value for radium halos on the black market. It was fairly undocumented and he planned to dig around today to see what he could find out.

He did tell me what he knew. Which was next to nothing.

"So people do know about it," I had said to him. "And there's a spot for it in the black market? Why?"

"Probably because people want superpowers," he said dryly. "Although I don't know how they would transfer it over. I'll have to do more tests."

"What's the danger level?"

"Zoe," he said. "Don't treat this lightly. If that druggie is to be believed, the blood in you is worth millions."

I shuddered at the memory. I didn't even want to think about what would happen to me if some sick freak got a hold of me for my superpowers.

"Hey, Zoe," Brent said, falling into step with me. "You okay?"

"Yeah. Apparently we're meeting after school at your place, by the way. There's something Heidi needs to tell us."

"Is this about the robbery?"

"Yes and no," I said. "I already know what it is, and so does Seth, but I can't tell you here. We'll fill you in when we get to your place."

"Is it bad?"

"So bad," I said. "My dad almost didn't let me go to school."

"*Dr. Landers* knows?"

"I'll fill you in when we get home."

"No." Brent shook his head. "I'm not waiting for school to finish. Go get Heidi and I'll find Seth. We're leaving now. This shit needs to end now. Rylee's dead, Kieran's in jail, we're being followed and blood's being stolen from us. There's too much stuff. It's going to explode."

I looked around to see if anyone had stopped to listen to him. No one had. It was a typical Monday morning with students still half-dead to the world. "Meet me outside in ten minutes."

I found Heidi at her locker and slipped my arm through hers. "We gotta go. Now."

She slammed her door and moved immediately beside me, not saying a word.

Brent and Seth showed up two minutes later. Everyone climbed into the Beetle. Heidi and Seth in the back, Brent in the passenger seat. We all scrunched down as I pulled out of the school parking lot, half-expecting a teacher to appear and stop us. Nobody did.

None of us said anything until we were nearly at Brent's.

"Kieran's in jail." I glanced in the rear-view mirror.

"We know." Seth met my gaze. "Brent told us last night."

"Oh." I shot a quick look at Brent. "He called our house last night. Somebody knows about the radium halos."

"We know." Heidi pointed to her head. "Someone tried to drink my blood yesterday."

Brent swung around. "Really?"

"I swear, if someone asks me if I'm dating Heidi one more time, I will punch them," Seth said suddenly.

"Heidi," Brent said. "Are you dating Seth?"

Seth punched him in the arm. "You're an asshole."

"What?" Brent asked, laughing. "I asked Heidi."

"I support the punch," Heidi said. "Now get out, we're here."

I turned the car off and hopped out of it, pulling the seat back so Seth could get out. Thank goodness Brent knew how to make us laugh. I had a killer headache itching to drive me crazy at the back of my head.

We headed inside the gym and followed Brent single file to the boardroom-turned-our-campout.

"We are apparently worth a lot of money."

Everyone stopped and turned to look at me.

"Pardon?" Brent asked.

"Black market and who knows what the hell else." I sighed. The secret was out and someone would figure it was the five of us.

"So what's with this black market thing?" Brent sat down on a leather chair at the table.

"It's the radium halos," I said quietly and sat across from him. "It's in our blood, creating radium halos. We're worth the price of Hawaii. Well, one of us is."

"How do you know that?" Seth asked.

"They threw the druggie you beat up into the same cell as Kieran. He told Kieran everything and Kieran used his one phone call to call my dad."

Brent shut his eyes and rubbed his temples. "Wait. Back up a sec. What the hell happened? The druggie that robbed the store knows we have radium halos in our blood?"

"He knows I have radium halos," Heidi said. "He might figure Seth does too, but he doesn't know about the two of you." A visible shudder went through her body. "He knew what I was because of my blood. My head hit a display case and he touched the blood running from it and then said it was radium halos. He said I was going to make him rich."

"And he just happened to tell Kieran, who just happened to be sharing a cell with him?" Seth grunted. "Why am I not surprised?"

"This can't be happening." Brent dropped his head into his hands. "You're going to need some sort of protection, Heidi. If he told Kieran after knowing him for a few minutes, then who knows who else he's going to tell. Or how long he's going to be in jail."

"There's no protection detail we can hire," Seth said. "What are we going to say? We have superpowers so we need bodyguards to keep people from selling our blood? Do you want us all to get committed?"

"I didn't say we should tell the truth," Brent argued and slapped his hand on the table. "But she should be protected. So should you. Both of you were involved in an armed robbery. That's reason enough to get protection on you."

"The druggie has no friends or any real connections to speak of aside from his dealer, who is now also in jail," Heidi said. "Officer Davis called me this morning to tell me the good news. So any chance of getting police protection is off, especially with them being understaffed as it is. And I can't really afford hiring a bodyguard."

"I can," Brent said.

"Brent." Heidi shook her head. "The last thing we need is to stand out even more. All of us have been in the middle of a lot of trouble, lately. If we stand out any more in that way then more than a druggie who saw me bleed will know that something is special in us."

We all stared at her. None of us had ever doubted that Heidi was smart, but she was absolutely right on this.

"We need to lay low," I said. "How're we going to stay under the radar when we're trying to find Rylee's killer?"

"And being followed?" Brent added.

"We're being followed?" Seth roared. "Since when?"

"A gray car. I don't know how long." Brent waved his hand. "I haven't seen it lately."

"I did." Brent glared at me in surprise when I admitted it. "Yesterday. I went to go talk to Kieran yesterday morning and then he was arrested. I saw the gray car parked in the motel lot where Kieran was staying. I tried to chase it down."

"What the hell, Zoe!" Brent stared at me from across the table. "Are you trying to get yourself killed?"

"We can't put the investigation on hold," Seth interjected. "We just can't."

"We can't get noticed by the next person looking for a fix, either," I said.

"Or a gray car trailing us." He got up and checked the hallway. "I'm going to reset the gym alarm. We'll be fine in here." He flipped open the switch by the door and set it. "We have to be careful. Even more than careful."

"How do we do that?" Seth said. "I'm already looking over my shoulder like a paranoid lunatic."

"We'll have to use our senses more. Even in public," I said. "See if anything is wrong or out of place. If we can detect it then we'll have more reaction time before they stuff a chloroform rag in our mouths."

"How are we going to do that?" Seth said. "I don't know about the rest of you guys, but I can't smell malicious intent."

"We'll have to train our senses harder," I said. "And we're going to have to really get back into training for fighting. Even more."

"I'll talk to my dad," Brent offered. "It won't be hard for me to guilt him into letting me using the gym again. Hell, I might even be able to get my own martial arts instructor."

"A martial arts instructor would be cool," Seth said. "It's like we're really training. Wax on, wax off, and then suddenly we're all badass."

"I don't think that's totally how it works," Heidi laughed and then quickly turned serious again. "I'm sorry. This is serious."

"I'm heading to the gym." Seth turned to go. "Anyone else want to go?"

"I haven't talked to my dad yet." Brent stepped in front of the door to stop him. "We're technically not supposed to be in there."

"Yeah, but that was because we moved things around," Seth said. "We'll just keep things as they are right now and run laps or something. I think all of us need to blow off some steam. Am I right?"

We all nodded, even Brent. "Let's go," he said and turned the alarm off again.

We headed to the gym and ran laps, which eventually turned into a game of tag when Seth slapped Brent on the shoulder as he passed him in a lap. "You're it!" he shouted.

"No way." Brent ran straight for me and I dodged, running behind Heidi, who Brent slapped on the shoulder. "You're it."

Heidi laughed and turned a sharp turn to run into Seth. "Not anymore," she said.

We played tag like third graders at recess after having a box of doughnuts. It was perfect. Nothing was wrong with the world when we played. We were just a group of kids from Elliot Lake again, even if we were sprinting faster than most humans would ever do in their life, and for a much longer time. There wasn't any killer picking us off and there weren't prices on our head for our blood. And we definitely weren't fighting anymore.

After several hours, we collapsed in the middle of the gym floor, exhausted and breathing hard. I could hear everyone's racing heartbeats gradually slow down.

"That was fun," Heidi said. "We should do that more often."

Seth smiled. "Yeah," he said. "Next time I'll totally win."

"No one really wins, Seth." Brent laughed. "It's tag."

"Actually everyone wins. Except Seth, because he's it." I giggled as he reached out and tapped me on the shoulder.

"Not anymore, Zoe," he said. "Now you're it. I win."

"Whatever you say."

We all stared up at the ceiling above. It was a high ceiling covered in stadium lights that were, thankfully, turned off. I reached out and touched Brent's fingers and he grabbed my hand. I turned my head to find him smiling at me.

"Hey, guys, we all see you," Seth chuckled. "Get a room."

I flipped over onto my stomach and stuck my tongue out at him. "Where do you and Heidi have yours?"

He growled but quit teasing.

Slowly reality settled back in.

"My mom's going to shoot me for skipping school," Heidi moaned.

"My dad'll have my hide," Seth sighed.

I sat up. "We're all going to be okay. One way or another, we're going to get out of this just fine."

Chapter Twenty-Four

"Through high transfugal force, the radium in your blood can be separated from your blood cells," Dad told me. "So theoretically, it's possible to filter it all out and you'll be a normal human again."

I bit my lip, thinking about it. After playing tag earlier that day, I'd headed straight to Dad's office. I knew I didn't want my superpower to be separated from me anymore. It was pretty cool listening to conversations whispered down the hall from me and knowing how many people were walking behind me and what the teachers really talked about in the teacher lounge. But I knew it was necessary for me to get rid of it if I ever wanted to live a normal life again. "What do you think I should do?"

"I think you could get rid of it, Zoe-zey," my dad said. "The existence of the radium halos in your blood is a scientific marvel that was never thought possible before. Having the honor of studying it is like a dream come true to me. But more than anything I want my daughter to be safe, and not hunted down."

I nodded. "I'm just not sure anymore. I need to tell the others, though. They deserve to know so they can make the decision to get rid of it if they want to. Can I think about this?"

He nodded. "It's a big decision, Zoe-zey. You need to give it a lot of thought. You already know my opinion. Talk about it with your friends, even Kieran if you have to. But make sure you go with what you want to do, not anyone else. I still don't know if it's possible to get the powers back through a blood transfusion or not. Even if I could, though, the amount of radium would be diluted and the powers weak."

"Okay. We just want the craziness to end. We never asked for any of this."

He nodded. "I know."

I moved toward the door.

"Can you tell Eleanor to call in my next appointment?"

"Will do," I said. "See you tomorrow, okay? Remember, I'm spending the night at Mom's."

His eyes dilated slightly at the mention of Mom, but less than usual. He was slowly growing used to being divorced with her, but I knew it still bothered him. "Okay," he said. "See you tomorrow."

I headed down the hall.

Eleanor sat flipping through a magazine at her desk. She was holding it far away with a frown on her face as if she had a headache and I briefly wondered if she had gotten new contacts before realizing I didn't care enough to even ask her. "You can send in the next appointment," I said.

She nodded and gestured to the mother and son sitting in the waiting room to go in. "Zoe," she said as I reached the door. "Can you kill that fly on the wall? Near the painting of the lake."

I looked over at the housefly, grabbed a magazine, rolled it up and hit the fly before it could escape. I looked at Eleanor. She was watching me from her desk, which was at least ten feet away. "How did you see the fly from over there?"

She looked at me like I was an idiot. "It's been buzzing around for the past half hour. I tried hitting it with this magazine but couldn't catch it."

I raised an eyebrow. When did she ever take her face out of a magazine long enough to watch a fly buzzing around the waiting room? "Well, have a good day, Eleanor."

"You too, Zoe."

I left, wondering if Dad had talked to his nurse about her people skills and if she had actually listened.

Mom was in the kitchen when I came home. "Hi, sweetie," she said. "I'm making lasagna for dinner. Why did your father want to see you after school today?"

"Huh?" I asked, paranoid she was testing me about skipping school. Her heart rate showed no sign of hiding anything. "Oh, nothing. I just left something at his house."

She raised an eyebrow. "That was a pretty long visit in the middle of his work day for something that you supposedly left at his house."

"He's my dad," I said. "We talk from time to time."

"He used to be my husband," she muttered. "And he always kicked me out of his office whenever I stopped by, no matter what the reason was. Zoe, is there anything at all wrong?"

"No, Mom," I said. "Nothing's wrong. Believe me."

"Are you sure?" she said. "Ever since you and your friends got trapped in the mine, you have been acting strange and getting into more and more trouble. Now, after Rylee's death, I'm..." She closed her eyes. "I'm scared I'm losing you, Zoe. You've changed and I'm not sure it's for the better."

I got up and kissed her cheek. "Nothing's changed, believe me. It's still me."

That part wasn't all a lie. I was still me. I was just a different me.

She looked at me skeptically. "Are Seth and Heidi dating now?"

I grinned. Take it from her to smoothly change the subject. "I think they really do like each other." My grin turned into a smile. I wasn't going to get caught for playing hooky. The school had miraculously let it slide. "He did break into a jewelry store to save her, after all, and Heidi has been spending a lot of time getting Seth over Rylee's death."

Mom shuddered. "I still can't believe he risked his life like that. Please promise me you'll never do that for anyone, not even for me or for your dad. The last thing I need to worry about is your safety. Understand?"

She had no idea. It was probably better that way. I crossed my fingers behind my back. "I promise. I won't do anything risky like that at all." *Unless someone I love is in trouble. Then everyone needs to get out of my way.* "How much longer until dinner is ready?"

"It won't be for another half hour. Why don't you go get started on your homework and I'll call you in when it's ready, okay?"

"Okay." I felt heat burn on my cheeks. What homework?

"And don't watch the news while you do it."

I rolled my eyes. "It helps me focus. You think I'm actually interested in the new policies involving fishing limits in the lake?"

She looked at me sourly. "On second thought, you might learn something from the news. Like how the policies will impact the economy and the environment, and how that actually makes some of your classes useful despite what you think."

I grinned. "Gotcha! I'll pay very close attention to that, then." I knew exactly what to say to get my way with things like that. Even if I really didn't give a damn about the policies. It was other news that I was more concerned with. News that was guaranteed to be playing tonight because it was so big in the quiet town of Elliot Lake.

I got out my textbooks and notebooks and spread them out on the living room floor like I was actually studying before turning on the TV.

"...Kieran's trial will be held later this week," the news reporter was saying. "After speaking with national officials, it has been decided that because of the nature of the crime, Kieran will remain in United States custody for the time being. DA officials have released that there is a possibility of a deal being in the works for Kieran because of his age and extenuating circumstances, but they have refused to give specifics. In other news..."

I tuned it out, thinking about what the reporter said. A deal? Why? Yes, he had been acting in self-defence, but he had also run from the police and had stolen police files. What type of deal would they give him? Unless they hoped he would be helpful in finding Rylee's killer. He did know about the location of the car, and the pictures of the crime scene as well as the key from the car would have been found in his motel room. The death of a young girl would definitely have higher priority than an old drunk who was killed in self-defence.

I felt hope welling up inside of me and I crushed it back down. Talk of a deal didn't mean he had immunity or even that he could stay in the States. Hell, he hadn't even taken the deal as far as I knew. But there was at least a chance of a lighter sentence. Maybe even some of the more minor charges would be dropped. That made me happy.

I needed to tell Kieran there was a way to get rid of the powers. I wasn't sure if he wanted that or not, but he deserved to know. He was going to get hunted like the rest of us if he was ever discovered. And if he ended up in jail, what were the chances that he wouldn't ever bleed in front of a criminal, or the prison doctor didn't know about the urban legend?

I doubted Kieran could take visits and even if he could, my parents would not let me visit the jail, even if it is just to talk to Kieran. Not even my Dad would be okay with that. But I'm sure if I got a message to his lawyer, then he would be able to pass it on to Kieran.

A quick Google search got me the name of the public defense attorney that was managing Kieran's case. I got the address of his office building and decided to make a stop by there tomorrow with a letter he could pass on to Kieran.

Chapter Twenty-Five

I smoothed down my blouse nervously. I didn't know what the rules were for meeting the defense attorney of your soon to be ex-boyfriend, although I doubted I would actually get an audience with the lawyer himself. Weren't they always busy? I figured I would have more luck if I looked presentable, so I dressed in my good white blouse and gray slacks.

"You sure you don't want me to go in with you?" Brent asked. "Just for moral support?" He was riding shotgun so he could watch the car while I was inside, and provide backup if trouble started.

This was the kind of life we were living now. "I'm just dropping off the letter." I looked down at the envelope in my hands. More than anything, I was wondering if the lawyer would open it and read it, or someone else would before Kieran saw it. Most likely he didn't know what radium halos were. Even if he did, he was bound by law to keep it confidential, right? I couldn't convince myself to trust anyone anymore. Public defense attorneys didn't make that much money. That didn't make him crooked, but I couldn't help but wonder.

"It's going to be fine," Brent said. "You know you need to get that letter to Kieran. He has as much thinking to do about it as the rest of us, even if it would be harder for him to get the treatment than us."

I nodded as I stared at the old brick building that was set in downtown Elliot Lake. The courthouse was connected to the building as well. "Okay. I'm going to go in. Keep an eye out, and if you see anything suspicious, drive to our second location and text me."

"Will do."

I got out and went into the building. The office building was ancient and the layout of the interior had been changed a thousand times over, but never all of it at the same time, creating a maze of hallways and the guarantee of getting lost if your destination wasn't right inside the door. Even following the maps on the wall, it took me half an hour to find the defense attorney's modest office, leaving me feeling slightly stupid and probably looking a little worse for wear.

Mr. Stephen Strayer was a middle-aged man with a haggard face and premature silver hair. He had gone to a state university to get his law degree and did only okay on the bar exam, which made it next to impossible for him to get a job at a decent law firm. Instead he became a public defense attorney for a wage that probably barely covered his bills and student loan payments.

I shook my head. I'd made all these assumptions based on what? His diploma?

There wasn't even a secretary to field appointments. I found him in the small office looking over a file. I knocked on the side of the door. "Excuse me, Mr. Strayer?"

He looked up and blinked. "Yes? Do I know you?"

"No, but are you representing Kieran?"

He sat up and surveyed me with some more interest. "I am. Are you a friend of his?"

"Yes," I said. "I was wondering if you could get a letter to him."

"Of course." He stood and walked around his desk. "You understand he won't be able to keep the letter of course, but I can arrange a meeting with him and let him read it."

I nodded. "That'll have to do." I handed him the letter and turned to go, but then paused and turned back. "This is rude, but you're not going to look inside, right?"

"I do my best not to invade my client's privacy," he said, the envelope securely in his hands. "If I have to look at it, I'll keep it completely confidential. However, for my own peace of mind, can I ask—" His face reddened and he rubbed his eyes. "It's not pictures, right? Please tell me it's not pictures of..." He trailed off and I blushed.

"No! Nothing like that!" My voice rose an octave. "It's personal stuff, but not like that or anything about why he's in jail." I was babbling, thrown off about the picture thing.

Mr. Strayer held up his hands. "I just had to make sure. You would be surprised at the contents of some of the messages I've been asked to pass along."

"Well, I can assure you it's just a letter. And totally innocuous, okay?"

He nodded. "If that's all, then have a good day."

"How is he doing?"

"Kieran?" He scratched his head, as if trying to remember. "He's all right. They had to put him in a single cell. He was threatening to hurt his inmate." He shook his head. "The boy is quite the puzzle."

"He's been through a lot." I swallowed, not wanting to say too much. "Is he allowed visitors?"

"Not at the moment. Give it a few days and check back with me, Miss... I'm sorry, I don't know your name."

"Zoe Landers."

He smiled. "I'll pass on your message, Miss Landers."

"Thanks." I turned to go, thankful I hadn't heard my phone vibrate and thankful that Mr. Strayer's body language, his heart rate and everything showed him to be a decently honest guy. He hadn't lied when he said he wouldn't read it, and his heart had jumped nervously when he mentioned the photos. For once, something was going in the right direction.

"Stay in touch, Miss Landers. That boy needs all the help he can get."

I nodded, not sure how to respond. I left and walked out of the building to find the car gone just as my phone buzzed.

Gray car came by. I'm trying to find it. Walk home by the back roads and keep listening. Be careful. Brent.

I sighed and pocketed my phone. It was a forty-five minute walk home or a twenty minute jog. It wouldn't be that bad if I was going with someone or I didn't have to look out constantly for possible attackers. But as it was right now, it was only bearable. I just hoped Brent followed his own advice and was careful himself.

I didn't worry about ruining my nice clothes as I started jogging down a back road behind the office building. A twenty minute run would barely make me break a sweat, especially on an overcast day like today. I did worry that it would look weird for someone in dressy clothes to be running. However, I didn't want to be vulnerable and on my own more than necessary.

I opened myself up to the world around me, taking in all of the sounds from the thunderous roar of the traffic on the road to the scratching sound of a nearby mouse scavenging scraps from a dumpster. Taking in the sounds around me like this no longer gave me a headache, which I was grateful for. As I jogged, I focused on trying to learn as much as I could from that around me. I might not be able to hear malicious intent, but after practicing I might be able to know when something was suspicious.

I got back to my mom's safely and I sent Brent a quick text to say I was home and going to lie down. My head was killing me.

It took a bit to fall asleep and when I finally did, it felt like I'd only slept a moment before my mom poked her head into my room. "Zoe?"

"Yeah?" I mumbled, trying to figure out what time it was by the darkness outside. I'd slept longer than I thought.

"You all right?"

"I'm fine." I sat up and rubbed my eyes. I heard another person breathing and an increased heart rate.

Mom's cell phone was pressed to her shoulder to try to mute the mike. "You haven't heard from Brent lately, have you? His mother's on the phone right now and apparently he hasn't come home."

Chapter Twenty-Six

Brent

I shifted, trying to shake the sluggish, heavy feeling inside my head. What the hell had happened? The last thing I remembered was waiting in the car for Zoe to come out and seeing the gray car and driving after it. Then... nothing.

I tried to sit and panicked when I realized I was strapped down to a table. I screamed, but it was muffled by duct tape covering my mouth. Thrashing was useless.

"Relax, Brent," someone said.

The voice sounded vaguely familiar but I couldn't place it anywhere. It was feminine. One of my mom's friends?

"The more you struggle the more your blood will flow and I can't have any of that precious liquid wasted, can I?" The woman moved into view with a piece of gauze.

Pain zinged through my arm as I tried to move. I glanced down at the needle and back at the woman, my blurry vision clearing. I stopped thrashing when I recognized who she was. Eleanor, Dr. Landers' nurse. She pressed the gauze to a small cut on the inside of my other elbow. A needle prick, I realized. I started struggling again.

"You're not going to get free," Eleanor tutted. "I'm very good at tying knots." She smiled at me, a weird gleam in her eyes. "It's just my luck, you know? That you have O-negative blood. Do you know what that means?"

It meant I was compatible with every type of blood type out there. It was very valuable at blood drives. It also meant that the radium halos in my blood could be transferred to anyone in the world. *Shit!*

"You know, Brent?" Eleanor smiled and stuck a syringe into the muscle on my bicep. "When I realized the five of you had radium halos in your blood, I was ecstatic. At first I only thought it was Zoe. Then I knew the rest of you had it, and Kieran too. He fooled me." She tutted again. "He switched his blood or knew how to hide the result from Dr. Landers." She shook her head. "I promise I won't go easy on him. I know how you all feel about him."

She glanced at the bag of blood hanging beside me. "One full, and another already on the way. The needle here will help you relax." She rubbed her hands together.

"You won't get away with this." The drug she'd just pumped into me confused my thoughts and made it hard to focus. I tried to use my hands to see instead.

She tilted her head as if listening to something. "I have a secret to share with you." She leaned down close to my ear. "It just so happens Rylee has the same blood type as me." She squealed and I jerked my head away from the noise. "When Dr. Landers started going down to his basement lab I knew something was up. I snuck in and checked his files, copied them and googled what I didn't know."

"You bitch!"

"I tried to get Rylee to get in the car with me," she continued, ignoring me. "But the little snot wouldn't listen. I only meant to tap her with the car to knock her out. The stupid snow!" She hit her head with the heel of her hand. "Stupid! Stupid! Stupid!" She dropped her hand and sent a nut-job smile my way. "Since I wasn't able to kidnap her, I did the next best thing. Then it only took a couple of paltry bribes to see the body before it was embalmed to get what I needed. Now, many experiments later, I have a new pair of eyes." She fluttered her eyelashes. "I can see everything, Brent! Rylee made me special."

I thrashed, trying to break free and knowing it was futile.

She ran a finger down the side of my face. "You, handsome, are going to give me another strength, and then you're going to make me rich." She picked up a syringe and pressed the plunger all the way down before sticking it into my arm and drawing blood into a vial. There were another twenty or so vials lined up on the table beside her.

Chapter Twenty-Seven

Zoe

"I can't find him anywhere!" I'd called Seth and Heidi immediately and went out to meet with them. I left a message with my dad as well. "Have you guys found anything?"

"His car," Heidi said. "It was in a ditch outside of town. Judging by the marks on the road, he swerved to avoid something."

"Another freakin' trap," Seth growled. "Where the hell are we going to find him?"

"Somewhere." I grabbed my car keys. "Let's go check his car and see if we can find any sign of who took him."

It was after midnight and every sane person was basically sleeping, in their homes or doing anything but hanging at the edge of down. The three of us were too wide awake and scared to even think about sleep. Brent's parents might have to wait forty-eight hours before they could fill out a missing person's report, but we weren't going to wait. After combing through the town, the car was our only clue.

We drove and parked just behind Brent's car. All of us jumping out and racing to it. My stomach twisted in a knot as I forced myself to keep my pace moderate. Every second we wasted meant one more second Brent was in danger, but we also needed to save our energy if we were to be of any use in saving him.

We shined our flashlights on the car. The front end was crumpled from falling into the ditch and covered in mud. The ditch was deep enough to hide the car from the view of passing drivers, which explains why no one had found it yet. Or the police had not had it towed. We went down the steep slope carefully before landing on the car.

"Look at that!" Seth pointed the beam of his flashlight to long marks in the ground going away from the car. "Something was dragged out of the car."

Brent. "Can you see any footprints?" I asked.

He knelt down and examined the ground up close. "Nope. Not clear ones, anyway. I'm thinking whoever it is had small feet. I'm guessing a woman. I can smell something sweet."

Heidi gagged. "I can taste it."

Seth straightened and shined his flashlight up the steep slope to the road. "She probably dragged him out of his car up the hill to her own car."

"You sure it was a woman?" Heidi said, going to the driver's side door of the car. I realized it was swinging open and my stomach tightened. "For a hill like that, it would take a lot of strength."

"What?" Seth said. "You don't think women are strong?"

"I don't think most men are that strong." She ducked her head into the car and quickly covered her mouth. "There's blood in here, guys." She gagged loudly. "It tastes awful."

"Brent!" I ran over to the car and shined my flashlight inside. There was a smear of blood on the cracked windshield. "Seth, get over here," I shouted.

He jogged over and pushed me aside. He and Heidi huddled in the doorway, taking in everything they could.

"There's no taste of sweat or nervousness," Heidi said. "He had no idea what was happening then. Probably passed right out."

"That sweetness I smelled wasn't perfume. It had to be something emitting from the kidnapper's body. Maybe it isn't a woman." Seth sniffed again. "I only smell a little bit of your perfume, Zoe, and Brent's aftershave in that regard. But whoever it is had definitely used hand sanitizer very recently."

"Do you think you could follow Brent's scent or the smell of the getaway vehicle, Seth?"

"I'm not a bloodhound, Zoe." Seth made a face. "My nose isn't that strong."

I groaned. "Damn it! Maybe we'll find something else that can at least point us in the right direction!"

But we couldn't find anything and we went home, exhausted and frustrated.

When I got home, I found Mom pacing the living room. "Where were you?" she asked, barely containing her anger.

"I was at Heidi's." I fidgeted. "She was freaking out about Brent being missing."

"And a simple phone call is too much to ask?" She raised an eyebrow at me. "You don't leave this house without telling me. Especially at night! I don't care how old you are!"

I clenched my teeth. I knew it was a bad excuse but there really wasn't any good reason for me to be out so late, especially on a school night. "We already lost one friend this year! I'm terrified I'm going to lose another. So excuse me for not thinking to call you!" I inhaled a sharp breath. "I left a message with Dad."

"You don't live with your father."

I glared at her. "Half the time I do! You think it's fair I have to tell both my parents every time I make a move? I didn't ask for this. I didn't ask for any of it and yet it's all thrown on me and I'm expected to act completely normal, like nothing's wrong. Bull shit!"

She stared at me with big eyes and her mouth hanging open. Her eyes softened and I'd managed to avoid an argument tonight. But then she closed her mouth in a tight set line. "I know it's been a rough year for you, but that's no excuse to be out past midnight and without my knowledge. Grief counselors recommend structure after a suitable time of mourning to help the grieving move on. Whether you're referring to your friend passing or my and your dad's divorce. Zoe, that time of mourning has passed. You're grounded."

"What?" I said. "That's not fair! There's no freakin' suitable time of mourning. Rylee was murdered! Who knows if Brent is next!" I clamped my hand over my mouth, terrified I'd said too much.

"You're grounded, young lady," she said. "Two weeks. I'll tell your father about all of this so don't think you'll get away with it at his place either." She covered her face with her hand. "Now go to your room and get some sleep. I'll take you to school in the morning."

I was totally screwed. We were all screwed. I covered my face with my hands. "I'm going to call Dad." I turned and stomped out of the room. My mom knew nothing. Nothing at all.

Chapter Twenty-Eight

Heidi and Seth were both as exhausted and nervous as I was the next morning. They met me in the school parking lot and gave me a cup of coffee. "I don't suppose you got a call from Brent last night," Heidi said. "You know, to the effect that he was run off the road, taken to the hospital and was unconscious for several hours but he's now awake and stable?"

"Nope." I shook my head. "Besides, my dad already checked the hospitals. He was up all night trying to find out anything he could."

"I knew it was a long shot." Heidi leaned against Seth, dejected. "You don't think he was taken out of Elliot Lake, do you? You don't think..."

"I sure hope not," Seth said. "How about one of us checks the car again now that it's daylight? One of us goes searching up in the mine and the woods, and one—"

"Sits in her father's office, helpless and upset because she was caught and grounded last night," I finished for him. "Sorry, guys. My mom's ticked."

Seth groaned. "Blow them off. We need to get Brent."

I shook my head. "My mom's being ridiculous. I'll talk to Dad. He'll be more understanding than Mom is, but the chances are still slim. If I blow them off, then something a lot worse than a grounding will happen." I knew my parents were very worried about me because of all of this. Dad understood, Mom knew nothing except I was skipping school and talking back.

"Go talk to your dad. He'll understand. Seth and I will go check Brent's car, tell his parents we found it and then also go check by the mine and forest." Heidi squeezed my hand. "We'll check back in at your dad's office if we find anything."

I nodded. We looked at the school building grimly. It had sucked enough to arrive there without Rylee. Without Brent, the sense of normalcy was completely gone. "We can do this," I said with fake determination. "And the two of you will get Brent back by the end of the day."

Chapter Twenty-Nine

Heidi

I insisted on taking the woods, telling Seth I would be safer there where nobody really went in the winter instead of on the side of the road. He wasn't happy about it and I knew he didn't believe my story because, after all, it was mostly bullshit. But he would be more help at the car than I would be. He could smell things that I couldn't taste, and he was better at identifying what he smelled. Besides, tasting Brent's blood made me feel creepy and nauseous.

We didn't have time to cover everything together. We could get more ground covered on our own.

I walked carefully over the roots to keep myself from tripping as I looked around. Every now and then I opened my mouth and breathed in to see if I could taste anything on the wind, but I picked up nothing but the normal smells of the forest. I walked up to the mine and decided to make that my starting place. It was the most likely place for Brent to be held captive. It was out of the way, old, and nobody ever wanted to go near it, especially after everything that had happened up there. There weren't any hunting cabins in the area or fishing shacks. So unless the kidnapper was parking Brent out in the open, he would be in the mine in this area.

I tried my best to breathe evenly as I approached the mine. You would think I would be over it already, but the mine still freaked me out. It was there where everything changed. We were trapped in that room. It was here that Kieran's father's body was found. It was here that our lives fell apart.

I ignored my fears and moved closer to the mine, steeling myself to the stenches seeping out of the mine.

It was re-blockaded from after the storm when we were trapped there. I went up to examine the new wooden boards blocking the mine securely. They didn't look tampered with. Just in case, I pressed my ear to the side in case I heard anything.

"There's my prize."

I swung around to see the druggie from the jewelry store. He stood grinning at me. His tremors had stopped and he looked stronger and more in control than during the robbery. He had gotten his fix. "I thought you were in jail," I said, stalling for time.

"I made bail. The promise of big money makes my acquaintances very motivated when it comes to giving me a hand." He laughed, an eerie hollow sounding noise. "You're easy, you know? All I had to do was stay downwind of you and follow you all the way from Elliot Lake." He stepped closer. "I knew I'd find you," he whispered. "Now you're mine."

I side-stepped him and bolted into the forest as fast as I could. I heard his footsteps crashing behind me so I kicked it up a notch, running faster than I had ever run before. I knew it would make me lose steam fast, but that was better than letting him catch me, which would happen if I stopped running or slowed down even the slightest. If I could get back in town, he couldn't stop me. There would be too many witnesses. I had speed, but the tree roots had other plans. I stumbled and fell, scrambling.

He grabbed my arm and pulled me down to the ground. I did a kip-up and punched him in the nose as hard as I could before I took off running.

"Bitch!" he shouted. "You're not getting away that easily." He tackled me from behind and pinned me down before I could hit him or get away. He held my hands pinned behind my back and I felt an old rope dig around my wrists.

I struggled but he was too heavy for me to shake off. An awful taste hit my mouth. He'd pulled something out behind me. Without seeing it, I knew it was a needle with some kind of drug in it. I struggled harder.

A sickening thump sounded behind me and vibrated through my body. The rope on my wrists went slack and the man fell forward on top of me, crushing me and filling my nose and mouth with the stench of bad hygiene and the cloying smell of drugs.

"Seth?" I pushed the man off of me and rolled over, scrambling to sit up.

"Heidi? Are you all right?" The vaguely familiar feminine voice threw me. "Let me help you up." Eleanor, Dr. Landers' secretary stood above me holding out her hand.

"Thanks," I said, taking her hand. "What're you doing out here?"

"I was just going for a hike." She glanced quickly around and then at the unconscious man beside me. "It's my day off. I heard you scream and came running. I hit him over the head with that log."

"Smart thinking." I stood and wiped off my pants and shirt. "Is he dead?"

She glanced down. "Not sure." She shivered. "I'm not into sticking around to find out."

"Me, either." I looked at the man lying unconscious on the ground and nodded. He was probably the person holding Brent. "We need to call 911." I pulled my phone out and frowned. No reception.

"How about we walk toward the road and see if we can get a hold of the police?" Eleanor glared at the druggy. "What a worthless piece of money spent."

"Pardon?"

She smiled. "I wanted to swear but Dr. Landers always says I can't around kids. So I make up little sayings to cover my need to swear. Bad habit, I know. Silly me." She wiped her hands. "Let's get going before he wakes up."

Once the police had him in custody, he could tell us where Brent was. I needed to call Seth and get a hold of Zoe – fast. Brent could be in serious danger. I nodded. "Sounds good."

Chapter Thirty

Seth

There really wasn't anything left at the car. I tried to look at the footprints to see if there was really anything I could make out, but aside from the size, there wasn't anything. The warm air had melted some of the snow. I even tried doing the bloodhound thing Zoe suggested, but Brent's smell ended at where he was put in the car and I couldn't discern the smell of the car from the thousands of other cars that had been on the road. I sighed and went back to see if I could find anything useful, even though I hadn't yet and I doubted I ever would.

A car driving by slowed. I heard the driver get out of the car and I made my way out of the ditch, ready to pretend it was me who needed help.

"Seth?"

I looked at the older version of Brent and grinned, pulling him into a man-hug. "Nate! What're you doing here? Aren't you supposed to be nursing off a hangover right now?" Nate was Brent's older brother who was attending college right now. Except he was driving a rental vehicle from the airport at the moment.

Nate grinned. "My parents called me about Brent so I took the first flight I could get on." He frowned when he noticed the car in the ditch. "I'm guessing you're looking for him yourself?"

"It beats sitting on my hands." I shrugged, not sure how much Nate knew. "I'm not losing my best friend." The words came out fierce but I didn't care.

"He's my baby brother. Maybe I can help you."

I couldn't use my power around Nate, but it was getting me nowhere anyway. An extra set of eyes couldn't hurt. "Sure! I've been all over this car. There's really nothing."

"Do you think he ran away?" Nate asked as we jumped into the ditch.

"Honestly, I think he was kidnapped." I ran my fingers through my hair, watching his face closely. "There's no reason he would run away. And if he did, he would have told one of us so we didn't worry. He would have taken the car, not crash it right outside of town."

"Who would kidnap him?" Nate asked.

I froze. "Good question!" I rubbed my hands together "My money's on whoever killed Rylee, kidnapped him."

While I continued looking in the car for anything, Nate examined the footprints and drag marks. "Whoever dragged him out of here was really strong unless Brent lost sixty pounds since the last time I saw him."

"Believe me, he didn't." I found Brent's wallet under the back wheel, half-hidden in the snow. I opened it up to find his ID, a credit card, social security card, and a hundred dollars all tucked safely away, untouched. "He would have taken this, though, if he ran away." I showed Nate it.

He whistled when he looked at all of it. "Remind me to tell Brent how stupid he is to carry all of this around with him. One pickpocket could totally ruin his life." He pocketed the wallet and looked at the ground, brow furrowed. "What's this?" he asked, kneeling down. He picked something out of the dirt, holding it between his thumb and index finger.

My heart sank when I saw it. A stethoscope. "No way." This couldn't be. I grinded my teeth together. *I told those guys tell Dr. Landers was a stupid idea.*

"What?" Nate asked.

"I'm pretty sure that belongs to Zoe's dad," I said angrily. "Which means that either Brent is a clepto, or Dr. Landers kidnapped him."

"That's impossible!" Nate stared at me like I was crazy. "Why would Zoe's dad want to kidnap Brent? He's a pretty cool dude."

I shook my head, betrayal and shock overwhelming every other emotion inside me. "It has to be him," I whispered. "There's no denying that fact."

Nate pulled out his phone.

"Let's go." I started up the hill.

Nate stuffed his phone in his pocket and hurried after me. "What're you going to do? Confront him?"

I remembered Zoe saying she was grounded and would be trapped at her father's office all day. Trapped with him. She was in danger too. "We have to," I growled. "Before he does something bad."

Chapter Thirty-One

Zoe

"Dad, I'm going across the street for a coffee." I grabbed my purse and slung it over my shoulder. "Do you want anything?"

"Sure. Grab me one too," he said, not even looking up from the Internet article he was reading. "If you're not back here in five minutes, I'm going to come looking for you. Keep your phone handy."

"I know," I grumbled. "I know."

"Look, Zoe-zey," he said, sighing. "I honestly don't want you grounded either because I think you would be better off helping your friends than sitting here. But you did go out without your mother's permission, and she had every right to ground you. I must respect your mother's wishes. I also want you safe. Being with me or your mom seems the safest place at the moment."

"Brent's missing. I need to find him."

"That's what we are trying to do here."

"And coming up with nothing!" I threw my hands in the air. "Three people looking are better than two," I snapped. "But whatever."

"It'll work out, Zoe," he called after me. "You'll see."

I knew he was right about me being grounded. I should be grounded, after all. But last thing I wanted right now was to be stuck doing nothing like I was right now. Every second was one less of Brent's life. *If...* I refused to finish the thought.

The line to pay at the Starbucks across the street was mercifully short. I hurried back, not wanting to be on my own and constantly glancing over my shoulder. I set my coffee on top of the stack of magazines I had put on the waiting room coffee table before giving dad his coffee.

"Thanks, Zoe-zey," He took a sip and grimaced.

"Oh crap. I forgot the sugar, didn't I?" My mind was fried today.

"It needs a tad bit." He smiled. "I think Eleanor has a bowl full of those little packets in one of her desk drawers. Can you grab me a couple?"

"Sure," I said. It was Eleanor's day off today, which I thanked my lucky stars on so we didn't have to sit in the waiting room together for hours on end in awkward silence. I doubted she wanted me to rifle through her desk for anything, even if Dad had asked me to, which almost made me enjoy opening up all of the drawers to look for a stash of sugar.

It was the third drawer I opened where I found the sugar packets. Right next to it was a set of keys. I froze when I saw the keys. All of them were painted in nail polish to make it easy to find each key. I picked up the keychain with a shaking hand.

"Zoe, did you find the sugar?"

"Yes," I called back. "Coming, Dad." I pocketed the keys and quickly went to give Dad the sugar. I watched him stir it and take a sip.

He smiled. "Perfect," he said. "Thank you."

I fidgeted, looking back out at the desk. I needed to find more information about Eleanor to see if she was really the killer. "I was wondering... does Eleanor need her keys? Because I found them in her desk drawer."

"She usually walks to work, so I didn't know if she forgot them here on purpose or not."

I held them up and put on my best concerned face, which wasn't hard, because I *was* concerned. For Brent.

He looked at them, his brow furrowed. "Well, I'm assuming she left them here on purpose if she didn't need them. But that does look like a house key. How about we run over and ask her? She only lives a few blocks away."

I nodded. "Do you have her address? I don't know what her house looks like."

He looked up the address on his computer.

"How about I go on my own? Then you can keep researching radium halos."

He pressed his lips together before handing me a sticky note with the address scrawled on it with barely legible handwriting. "Okay. Just remember—"

"Yeah, yeah," I said, pretending to be annoyed. "If I'm not back in ten minutes you'll call the Secret Service and all that jazz."

"Well, calling you would probably suffice," my dad said dryly. "Worst case scenario, the Elliot Lake Police Department."

"I know, but the Secret Service would be so much cooler and make for a much better story." I ran over and kissed him on the cheek, leaving him with a surprised look and dashed out of his office and the building. I raced down the street, following the street signs and numbers and trying to read my dad's handwriting. If I hadn't spent over a decade learning to read doctors' handwriting, it definitely would have taken me more than ten minutes just to find Eleanor's place.

Eleanor's house looked so normal. Living in the suburbs of Elliot Lake—the closest we ever got to city living in this town—she had a small yard that was neatly mowed with a couple of empty flower beds in front of her windows. There was a tree in the backyard that might be an apple tree, but it was dead right now from winter. Her white house was shuttered and looked shut down, as if giving the resident privacy and blocking out the rest of the world. It also could mean she was hiding a secret she didn't want the rest of the world to know about.

There was no car in the driveway. The garage door was closed as well, but I cautiously walked up and looked through the windows.

I dropped the keys and bent down to quickly pick them up.

Inside the garage was a sporty, gray car.

I grabbed for my phone with shaking hands, but it slipped out of my hands. I caught it just before it hit the ground. I called Heidi. The phone rang and rang.

As I tried again, I hurried to the house and tried the door. It was locked. Ear to the door, I listened inside, hoping to hear anything to reassure me Brent was inside, alive. Nothing. There was complete silence inside the house except the ticking of a clock and the buzzing of lights.

Heidi's phone went to voicemail again. Being in the woods, she probably didn't have service. I swore silently and then tried Seth's phone.

"Zoe!" an overly cheerful voice said from behind me. "What're you doing here?" Eleanor had appeared behind me, looking at me with a smile that looked more like a threat than a sign of friendliness.

Seth's phone went to voicemail. I slowly hung up and put the phone in my pocket before holding out the keys. "Dad saw you left these at the office. He asked me to put them in your mailbox."

She stared at the keys and her face turned even colder. "Ah yes," she said, taking them. "If I remember correctly, those were in my desk drawer. What was your father doing looking through my stuff?"

"He needed sugar for coffee."

"And it was in my drawer." Eleanor laughed. "How's your search going for your friend? Brent? That's his name, right? I heard he was missing and that you had gotten grounded looking for him."

"It's going well, actually. I think I know *exactly* where he is."

"Really?" Anger and fear blazed in her eyes.

I steeled myself, more sure than ever now. Her body's reaction to my words gave away the secrets she was hiding. "Yes," I said, my eyes narrowing. "I have a pretty good lead."

"That's funny," Eleanor said as she pulled a gun out of her pocket and aimed it at me. "Because I also know where Brent is. Why don't I take you to him?"

Chapter Thirty-Two

Seth

Nate and I pulled up to the doctor's office and stormed in. We didn't bother knocking on Dr. Landers' door.

He looked up, surprised at us. "Seth, Nate, what are—"

I didn't give him time to answer. Instead I pulled him up out of the chair and slammed him against the wall. "Where are they?" I shouted. "I know you have them! Where are they?"

"I have no idea what you're talking about!" Dr. Landers snapped, trying to shove me away from him. He could barely move me.

Nate crossed his arms over his chest. "We found Brent's car, and we found your stethoscope right outside. It had to have fallen out when you were dragging Brent up the ditch to your car." He held up the dirty stethoscope as proof.

Doc's face paled and I was sure we had him, but then he started furiously shaking his head.

"No," he said. "That's Eleanor's stethoscope, not mine!"

"Why should we believe you?" I hissed. "A sociopath like you who's willing to kill innocent teenagers would throw anybody under the bus."

"I'm telling you, that's not mine." He held his hands up. "Nate, check my bottom right-hand drawer. You'll find my own stethoscope there. All of mine have my initials on them. Eleanor's probably does as well."

Nate went to the drawer anyway and pulled it out. "It's here," he said.

"Look at the metal ring," Dr. Landers said. "You'll find my initials engraved. Now look at the other stethoscope. You'll find that the initials don't match."

"He's right," Nate said. "This one says Eleanor."

Dr. Landers spun around when I released him. He paled. "I just sent Zoe over to Eleanor's house! Damn it!"

"Why would Eleanor be kidnapping Brent or Zoe?" Nate shook his head. "There must be a reason other than that she's crazy, right?"

Dr. Landers and I locked eyes and I nodded. We needed to tell him.

"I'll explain on the way," I said. "Let's go."

Chapter Thirty-Three

Zoe

I pulled my arm back and elbowed Eleanor in the face. The gun went flying and she spun around. I hit her again. She yelled out and grabbed her nose before punching me as hard as she could in the side of my head. Pain exploded in my temple and I realized she was much stronger than she looked. Suddenly the fly incident made sense. She had Rylee's power. Everything made a lot more sense.

But in the time it took for me to realize, Eleanor had punched me again and pulled me up by my arm and started pulling me into the house.

I struggled to get free. I grabbed her hand, pulling it out and twisting her arm until I heard a satisfying snap. She yelled out and yanked me back inside her house. "I never liked you, brat," she said through gritted teeth. "I'll make it much more painful for you than I did for any of your other stupid friends." She shut her front door, trapping me inside her house. She turned and swung her leg.

Suddenly everything went black.

I woke, a headache more painful than I had ever experienced pressed against my temples. I couldn't remember where I was. Carefully, I opened my eyes. The room was dark and windowless, lit only by a dim, bare, lightbulb hanging in the center of the room.

Eleanor! Everything came rushing back!

She was nowhere to be seen, but Brent and Heidi were both strapped down to tables, their heartbeats faint and slow, but they were still beating – for now.

I carefully tilted my head, trying to hear Eleanor in the house. Nothing.

The same room was soundproof.

That's why I couldn't hear anything before.

I wasn't bound. My head spun and my vision blurred, but I stood unsteadily and crawled over to Brent. His eyes were half-closed and he was pale. Too pale. I slapped him lightly across the face. "Brent," I whispered. "You need to wake up. Right now!"

He groaned and stirred slightly. His eyelashes cracked open as I started pulling at the ties binding him to the table. "Zoe?" he whispered faintly.

I saw him looking at me as his eyes tried to focus on me. "Let's get out of here."

His head fell to the side. "Heidi?"

"She's here too." I saw him staring at the table beside him. "Seth?"

"I don't know where he is right now. I'm sure he's getting help." It felt like forever to get Brent free, the knots were impossible to undo. I found a scalpel on an operating tray along the far wall and cut him loose. I tried to help him up, but he was dead weight against me. I kept the IV needle in him to keep him hydrated and hit the button to speed up the rate of the drip. I left him slumped on the table and checked Heidi. She had been here less time, maybe she could help me more.

I shook her awake and cut her free. She shot up, jumping off the table, ready to fight. She blinked and took a few seconds to focus on me. "Zoe!" She hugged me quickly. "Eleanor's the kidnapper! She killed Rylee!"

"I know." I nodded and turned back to Brent. "She got me too." I swallowed, wishing the pain in my head would go away.

"We need to get out of here right now! I need your help with Brent. He's in really bad shape."

Heidi stared at me. "You look in bad shape yourself."

"I'm fine."

"She's been draining his blood." Heidi glanced down at her arm. "She's going to do the same with me, and you. She's planning on selling it on the black market. I think she has powers too."

"She does. Rylee's power."

Heidi ran to the door leading out at the top of the stairs and tried it. "It's locked," she said and hurried back down. "Is there anything down there we can break the lock with?"

I looked around. I couldn't see anything right off. I checked my pockets, wondering if Eleanor could possibly be that stupid...

I pulled the keys out of my pocket. Apparently she was. I tossed them up to Heidi. "Try these." I went back to Brent, who was on the verge of losing consciousness again. "Brent, you have to stay awake. I'll get you to my dad as soon as possible but right now you have to help me." I grabbed his arm and put it around my shoulders and put my arm around his ribcage. I groaned as I hoisted him off the table and dragged him toward the stairs.

At the top, Heidi tried key after key. I heard the click before she noticed. "Got it!" she cried out and pushed against the door.

As soon as it flew open, a rush of noise came all at once, including Seth's voice and my dad's voice. "Help!" I shouted, dragging Brent slowly up the stairs. "We're down here!"

Heidi rushed back down to help me but I pushed her back up the stairs. "Get the others," I huffed. "The sooner my dad can look over Brent, the better."

She nodded and dashed up the stairs, leaving me to handle Brent alone.

He wasn't as heavy as Seth, but I had no idea how Eleanor was able to get him up the ditch and then down to the basement.

Even with the superhuman strength it would be a struggle. Unless she had an accomplice. The jewelry robber perhaps?

I heard everything upstairs like I was right there.

Heidi screaming for help as Seth and Nate struggled with Eleanor. I heard her cry out followed by a thump and I knew she was down, but her heartbeat said she wasn't dead. A second later both Seth and Nate rushed down the stairs to help me with Brent.

An ambulance was coming to the house, I could hear its siren. Dad stood waiting at the top of the stairs checking Heidi over. "Bring him to the kitchen and set him on the floor."

Dad hurried over and checked Brent's vitals. "He's lost a lot of blood. We need to get him to the emergency room now for a blood transfusion." He glanced up as the siren grew louder. "I already called." He stared at all of us. "He's going to be okay."

I breathed out a sigh of relief and almost collapsed against the wall as tension and anxiety left me. Suddenly, the headache in my head throbbed and threatened to knock me out. I slid against the wall to the floor, unable to stop the noise from everywhere explode in my ears.

Chapter Thirty-Three

Seth

It was over an hour before the doctor told us Brent was going to be okay. Aside from severe blood loss and a mild concussion from the car accident, he was going to be fine. Zoe lay resting beside Brent in the hospital room. She'd somehow been unable to control all the noise and damaged an ear drum. Well, that's what one of the doctors said and when he went to check it again, she was fine. She had a bad migraine they were medicating, but she was going to be okay also.

Heidi was fine as well. Eleanor had used chloroform to knock her out and the next thing she remembered was Zoe waking her up. Eleanor hadn't had time to drain any of her blood.

"You know, you can let me go," Heidi said. "I'm okay. Dr. Landers checked me out, remember?"

I reluctantly removed my arm from around her shoulders. "Sorry."

Heidi shrugged and then she smiled shyly. "I didn't say you had to let me go."

I smiled and put my arm around her shoulders again. She rested her head on my chest, her eyes closed. Even though she wasn't hurt, she was exhausted, and I didn't blame her. We all were. "When I realized you were in that basement..." I shook my head. Words didn't even begin to describe the terror I had felt. "I'm just relieved you're okay."

She smiled. "I like you too, Seth."

"Huh?"

"You know what I mean."

I smiled. Rylee had been sexy and glamorous, but I mostly liked her because she was out of my league and definitely not interested in me. Heidi was sweet. I could see myself with her forever.

I kissed her gently and she sighed, relaxing into me. It felt completely right, more right than anything else I had felt, and it was perfect.

Chapter Thirty-Four

Zoe

"How are you?" I asked as I stared at Brent lying beside me. My head no longer felt like it was exploding.

"Weak, human. Normal." He scoffed. "You're a sight for sore eyes."

I smiled. "I could say the same for you."

"I'm so glad it was me she kidnapped and not you," he whispered, running his fingers through his hair. "I wouldn't have been able to save you like you saved me. Hell, I wouldn't even be able to function if I lost you. You're really everything to me, Zoe."

I didn't know how to respond. I didn't want him to hurt, ever. I also wanted Kieran. I couldn't love both of them, it wasn't right. "I didn't deal with your disappearance very well either. Just ask Dad. I got grounded."

"Seriously?"

"Seriously. It's kind of embarrassing."

Nate knocked on the side of the door. "Am I interrupting something? Or can I see my little brother?"

Brent rolled his eyes. "Come on in."

He pulled up a chair on the other side of Brent. "So, you can see through walls, now."

Brent looked at me, his eyebrows high. "You the only one who knows? Or do all the doctors know?" Brent smiled sheepishly.

"Dr. Landers and Seth told me. No one else knows. But I'm repainting my room in lead paint."

"It's not going to work." Brent grinned tiredly.

He smiled. "Isn't that the only substance Superman can't see through? What if I bring a girl over?"

We all laughed. "I don't want to look into your room, bro," Brent said.

"Zoe? Brent?" Kieran stood at the doorway of the room, looking more put-together than we had seen him since before his father's body had been ID'd. He wore dark blue jeans and a clean t-shirt with his hair combed back and clean-shaven.

I kind of missed the scruff. My heart sped its rate and I glared at the monitor keeping track of it beside the bed. "Did you make bail?"

"No," he said. "I got a deal. I'm a criminal consultant. Kind of." He lifted up a pant leg to show a tracking anklet. "The police are interested in my psychic ability. That's what they're calling it." He winked at me. "Three years of good behavior and trying to help them solve some cases."

I held my arms open and he came over to hug me. "It could be worse."

"Yes," he said. "I've started the process to become an American citizen to help simplify the conviction process." He glanced at Brent and Nate, who were watching us intently. "Can I talk to you alone?" he asked.

"Yeah." I pulled the finger monitor off and slipped my feet out of the hospital bed.

"Careful, Zoe," Brent cautioned, his voice full of concern.

"I'll be okay." I slipped my arms through Kieran's and leaned on him as we made our way to the door.

We moved outside in the hall and closed the door to the room. No one else was around. We had complete privacy.

"I missed you," Kieran said. "I still do." He smiled. "Brent really likes you, you know. I knew that from the first day."

I blushed. "I know. I'm not sure what to do."

"You can't love both of us, Zoe."

I stared at the floor, unable to answer.

"I don't want you to wait for me, Zoe. I can't take care of you like Brent can." He smiled and lifted my chin with his finger. "I got your letter, by the way. I'm really glad it's possible to get rid of the radium halos. I don't want to now, obviously, but who knows after my sentence is up. Are you planning to do it?"

"I don't know." It was so dangerous having the powers. Eleanor was the tip of the iceberg of people who would covet something as unique and valuable as the radium halos. At the same time, it was pretty cool just having powers. I felt that as long as we all stuck together as a group, it would be okay. "I used to know, but everything's gotten really complicated."

He nodded. "I know."

I bit my lip. "I'm sorry. About everything."

"Zoe." He leaned close, our lips inches apart. "I love you more than anything. I always will. I want you to be happy. How can I make you happy when I really only have a mile radius from the police station? I can't take you on dates or cook for you anymore, not to mention help you train or even just be there for you."

"I loved you for so much more than that. You know that." I swallowed, my eyes falling to his lips.

"I know," he whispered, his voice breaking. "But if we stayed together it would just be ugly in the end." His lips touched mine.

Warmth shot through me. A delicious hunger licking at my insides begging for more. My hands found their way around his neck.

"Kieran!"

We pulled apart as a police officer at the end of the hall tapped his watch.

"Eleanor's in prison. She won't be coming out for a long time. Apparently she has to spend some time in the psych ward. She's been mumbling about radium theories and halos. Dr. Landers had to have her committed." Kieran grinned. "I've got to go." Kieran pressed his forehead against mine. "I just came along to see the end of this case through." He kissed my forehead.

He grinned as he started walking toward the police officer. "I'll be around." He turned and jogged down the hall.

It was over now. The first phase of my new life with radium halos was done, and hopefully the worst of the trouble was behind us.

All of us had changed since that fateful day in the mine. Not necessarily for the better. But all of us were stronger and less naive. We were more careful, as well as more alert. Time would heal and break us. And we would all go through it together.

The End
Conscience – Book 4 Coming Winter 2015/2016
Chapter 1 Excerpt Included!

BONUS EXCERPT!!

FIRST CHAPTER (rough draft) of the BOOK 4 IN THE
SERIES
Chapter One
Kieran

"All right, Scotland yard," Officer Davis said. "You've said goodbye to your girlfriend and you've closed the case. Time to go back to your cell."

"I'd appreciate it if you called me Kieran, officer," I said. "I'd hate to for see your death."

"I'd watch your mouth if I were you," he snapped, shoving me roughly in the direction of the cells. "You're just a glorified convicted killer whose now threatened an officer."

I clenched my jaw. *And you're a dickhead making racist remarks and practicing police brutality.* I wisely decided not to say anything though. Most of the officers at least didn't go out of their way to bully me, but Davis had been on a power trip since I was assigned to him a couple of days ago. Because I was considered a criminal consultant, I didn't have a partner like consultants do in TV, but I did have to have an officer responsible for me and Davis was less than happy about the arrangement so he was making me miserable. Or trying to, at least. I'm not sure I could feel any lower anyway after saying goodbye to Zoe, probably forever. Knowing she had moved on with Brent. I shuddered.

Davis led me down a hallway to what used to be an old storage room but what was now my new home. Elliot Lake didn't have the space to house long-term prisoners in the regular cells, especially ones who were best kept out of the way, like me.

Because of the radium halos floating in my blood, I was more valuable than an original DaVinci painting on the black market. That required more protection than what most of the prisoners had, so whether I liked it or not I got special treatment.

Davis unlocked the several locks on my cell door before opening it to reveal a small cot and thin blanket with a portable toilet chair right next to it. Aside from a small stack of books on the bed, it was depressingly empty. I wished more than ever that the story I told Zoe about being allowed to go wherever within a mile of the station was true.

Davis took off my tracking anklet and shoved me into the room before slamming the door. I sat down on my bed and looked at the books. While most convicts went to an actual prison and got access to a library among other things, I was able to check out three books per week from the public library to fill hours of free time. I had chosen two of the thickest novels I could find as well as a book on meditation and yoga. I had to learn how to control my power somehow. Even though some medical experts were being compiled to study me and help me, I needed to do something in the meantime. Random spurts of visions weren't going to help me if I was supposed to prove my value to the police.

I sighed and stretched before stripping off my t-shirt and tossing it on the bed before getting down on the floor and doing sit-ups. Working out would also help me keep my sanity for the next few years I would be stuck in here. However, as soon as my bare back touched the cement floor, I froze and closed my eyes. I was in a hospital room but I knew immediately it wasn't me but someone else's eyes I was seeing through. I was handcuffed to the bed, but only on one side. I reached up and grabbed a bobby pin from my hair and inserted it into the lock of the handcuffs. It only took me a second to be free. I got up as quietly as I could so I wouldn't tip off the police officer waiting right outside my room. I looked at the window. I was on the first floor of the hospital but the window was locked. I looked back at the police officer. I could see his chest moving up and down evenly and I knew that he was asleep. I looked around the room and grabbed the heart-rate monitor. I picked it up as carefully as I could and then slammed it through the window as hard as I could. Before the officer could even come into my room I was out the window and running as fast I as I could to the woods.

I jerked back to reality quickly and I was back on my back in my cell, breathing hard. I stood up and started pounding as hard as I could on my door. "Help!" I shouted. "Help!"

More by W.J. May

Rae of Hope
The Chronicles of Kerrigan

The Chronicles of Kerrigan

Book I - *Rae of Hope* is FREE!
Book Trailer: http://www.youtube.com/watch?v=gILAwXxx8MU
Book II - *Dark Nebula* is Now Available
Book Trailer: http://www.youtube.com/watch?v=Ca24STi_bFM
Book III - *House of Cards* is Now Available
Book IV - *Royal Tea* - Now Available
Book V - *Under Fire*
Book VI - *End in Sight,* Coming Fall/Winter 2015

More books by W.J. May
Hidden Secrets Saga:
Download Seventh Mark part 1 For FREE
Book Trailer:
http://www.youtube.com/watch?v=Y_vVYC1gve

<u>Book Blurb:</u>

Like most teenagers, Rouge is trying to figure out who she is and what she wants to be. With little knowledge about her past, she has questions but has never tried to find the answers. Everything changes when she befriends a strangely intoxicating family. Siblings Grace and Michael, appear to have secrets which seem connected to Rouge. Her hunch is confirmed when a horrible incident occurs at an outdoor party. Rouge may be the only one who can find the answer.

An ancient journal, a Sioghra necklace and a special mark force life-altering decisions for a girl who grew up unprepared to fight for her life or others.

All secrets have a cost and Rouge's determination to find the truth can only lead to trouble...or something even more sinister.

Shadow of Doubt
Part 1 is FREE!
Book Trailer:
http://www.youtube.com/watch?v=LZK09Fe7kgA

Book Blurb:

What happens when you fall for the one you are forbidden to love?

Erebus is a bit of a lost soul. He's a guy so he should be out to have fun but unlike the rest of his kind, he is solemn and withdrawn. That is, until he meets Aurora, a law student at Cornell University. His entire world is shaken. Feelings he's never had and urges he's never understood take over. These strange longings drive him to question everything about himself

When a jealous ex stalks back into his life, he must decide if he is willing to risk everything to be with Aurora. His desire for her could destroy her, or worse, erase his own existence forever.

Courage Runs Red
The Blood Red Series
Book 1 is FREE

Book Blurb:

What if courage was your only option?

When Kallie lands a college interview with the city's new hot-shot police officer, she has no idea everything in her life is about to change. The detective is young, handsome and seems to have an unnatural ability to stop the increasing local crime rate. Detective Liam's particular interest in Kallie sends her heart and head stumbling over each other.

When a raging blood feud between vampires spills into her home, Kallie gets caught in the middle. Torn between love and family loyalty she must find the courage to fight what she fears the most and possibly risk everything, even if it means dying for those she loves.

Free Books:

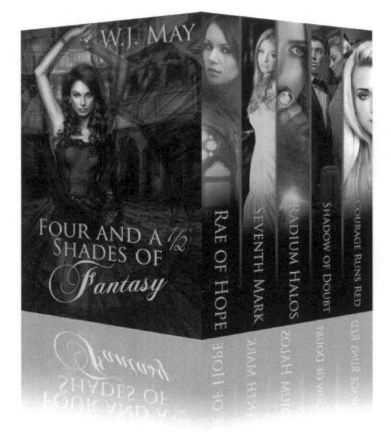

Four and a Half Shades of Fantasy

Did you love *Nonsense*? Then you should read *Courage Runs Red* by W.J. May!

What if courage was your only option?

When Kallie lands a college interview with the city's new hot-shot police officer, she has no idea everything in her life is about to change. The detective is young, handsome and seems to have an unnatural ability to stop the increasing local crime rate. Detective Liam's particular interest in Kallie sends her heart and head stumbling over each other.

When a raging blood feud between vampires spills into her home, Kallie gets caught in the middle. Torn between love and family loyalty she must find the courage to fight what she fears the most and possibly risk everything, even if it means dying for those she loves.

Fall in love with immortar vampires and werewolves in this paranormal fantasy series.